The Macat Library

世界思想宝库钥匙丛书

解析弗吉尼亚·伍尔芙
《一间自己的房间》

AN ANALYSIS OF

VIRGINIA WOOLF'S

A ROOM OF ONE'S OWN

Fiona Robinson Tim Smith-Laing ◎ 著

查诗怡 ◎ 译

 上海外语教育出版社
外教社 SHANGHAI FOREIGN LANGUAGE EDUCATION PRESS

MACAT

目　录

CONTENTS

引言

要 点

- 弗吉尼亚·伍尔芙是英国小说家和批评家，1882 年出生于伦敦，并在那里长大成人。她对文学和女权主义 * 理论的认知得益于其女性作家的丰富经验。女权主义是一项思想和政治运动，目的是寻求性别平等。

- 《一间自己的房间》于 1929 年出版。其创新点体现在作者关注并直面女性在日常生活中遭遇到的各种问题，关注到这些问题对女性思想的影响，而非关注那些法律方面的难题。

- 《一间自己的房间》在女权主义运动史上是十分重要的文本。无论在学术界还是在非学术界，该文本不断地吸引着读者，并持续地影响着女权主义文学批评。[1]

弗吉尼亚·伍尔芙其人

弗吉尼亚·伍尔芙，《一间自己的房间》的作者，1882 年出生在伦敦肯辛顿区一个高等知识分子家庭，并在那里长大。和她的几个兄弟不一样，她和姐姐瓦内萨从未上过中学和大学，而是在家里接受的教育。这一教育方式在当时比较普遍。虽然这给伍尔芙带来某些局限，但她所受的教育超越了大多数的同龄女性。伍尔芙的父亲是一名记者、历史学家和传记作家，家里藏书量可观，为她随心所欲地阅读提供了便利。因此，伍尔芙文学知识面广，这对她后来在学识上的精进功不可没。

---

[1] 学术界目前一般把20世纪60年代之前的"feminism"译作"女权主义"，而把20世纪60年代及之后的"feminism"译作"女性主义"，因此，文中的"feminism"和"feminist"也随着其指涉的时代而有不同的翻译。(译者注)

通过哥哥托比*和弟弟安德里安*的介绍，伍尔芙不到20岁就结交了一群知识分子、艺术家和作家。这群人后来以布卢姆斯伯里文化团体*而闻名。他们常常聚集在伍尔芙位于伦敦布卢姆斯伯里广场的家里。伍尔芙等好几位成员分别在艺术、文学和经济领域中谋求创新，引领发展的方向。他们思想独立，且十分前卫，反对当时许多惯性思维。

伍尔芙1915年出版了第一部小说，至1941年去世前，又出版了7部作品。她写完最后一部小说后不久便自杀，该小说在她死后才出版。伍尔芙的作品在当时甫一出版就获得成功，她被认为是现代文学界里一颗最为耀眼的星星。她去世后，声誉持续增长，她被公认为20世纪最伟大的小说家之一。

《一间自己的房间》的主要内容

尽管伍尔芙获得了成功和享有某些特权，但她仍然是一位生活在男性为主导的社会中的女性。她切身体验到20世纪初的英国社会给妇女设置的种种限制，这直接启发了她于1929年出版的散文集《一间自己的房间》。该作品围绕两个中心问题展开：历史上伟大的女作家为什么如此之少？女作家要写作，必须具备哪些条件？

伍尔芙首先回答了第二个问题。其中，标题已经回答了该问题的一个方面，即写作需要一间属于自己的房间；其次，钱是必不可少的，伍尔芙认为年收入必须有500英镑——这笔钱在1929年意味着生活既稳定又舒适。她认为，要写作就必须具备这些条件，因为写作是日复一日的事。要写作，必须有自己私人的空间，不能为钱而担忧。人只有在同时拥有私人空间和安全感时才能创造艺术。

伍尔芙的这一想法是对 20 世纪初期女性生活的直接反馈。尽管女性的法律权益逐渐扩大，但她们拥有的权益仍比男性要少。女性拥有个人资产和接受教育的权利仍然受到诸多限制。同时，社会对女性的期许也束缚了女性。女人社交的目的就是结婚，而一旦结婚，就不能再工作。女性一辈子就该相夫教子。因此，已婚女性不再拥有个人的收入，也不再享有个人的隐私。由此，伍尔芙提出上述两个基本要求，这在今天已是理所应当的事。

第一个问题——为什么伟大的女作家如此稀少？——更为复杂。20 世纪初，人们普遍认为女性智商比男性低，历史上鲜有伟大的女性作家和艺术家可作为证据证明该论点。然而，伍尔芙认为女性智商与男性一样，历史上鲜有伟大的女性另有原因。她提出，女性未能创作出伟大的作品，是因为她们受到了种种阻拦。

那么，是什么阻拦了她们呢？伍尔芙的分析是，社会自有史以来从未给女性创造能够写作的条件。女性没有自己的空间，没有自己的收入，也没有受到过教育。她指出，在这样的社会制度下，即便天赋超乎寻常的女性也无法创作。女性不创作文学，不是由于智力低下，而是被日常生活所干扰。

为什么当今没有伟大的女性作家？伍尔芙给出的第三个理由与从古至今伟大的女性作家一直缺席有关。她指出，前辈女作家的创作传统是当今女作家创作伟大作品的条件。为了创造女性创作的传统，她鼓励与她同龄的女性去创作，不论什么题材都可以。她认为只有这样，将来的女性才能创作出伟大的作品。

《一间自己的房间》的学术价值

《一间自己的房间》在女权主义发展史脉络中的重要性，想言过其实都难以做到。1929 年，伍尔芙在撰写该书时，英国的女性正处在一个转折点上：女性第一次拥有了选举权，她们正在冲破种种法定权限，争取着平等。但早期大部分的女权运动都仅专注于妇女获得法定权利。伍尔芙的这篇论文敏锐地发现并提醒世人，男女不平等除了不公正的法规，还有更深层次的原因。在她看来，女性社会地位低下影响到了她们生活的方方面面，并体现在日常的种种细微之处。《一间自己的房间》把女权主义活动的重心从争取法权转移到改变日常生活上来。

为了阐明这一点，伍尔芙集中阐述了文学批评上的一个核心问题：如何才能创作出好的艺术？ 20 世纪初，大部分学者和批评家都坚信只有"天才"能创造伟大的艺术。这样的"天才"能突破各种社会障碍。"天才"创造艺术、表达自我，可以超越贫穷、匮乏的教育，也不在乎是否有时间和私人空间。历史上伟大的女性作家和艺术家的缺席，正好可以证明女性不会成为天才。这也反证了视女性价值低于男性的社会结构是公正的。伍尔芙则另辟蹊径，转而关注日常生活是如何遏制了天才的创作。虽然她主要关注女性，但她的观点，即艺术紧紧地扎根于现实生活，引领了 20 世纪文艺批评的主要导向。《一间自己的房间》彻底打破了文学批评及其他领域的"艺术天才"观。

《一间自己的房间》出版至今已经过去了近 90 年，但其重要性依然不减。近一个世纪过去了，英国以及其他地区的女性生活都得到了改善，但伍尔芙的许多观点依然令人信服。她描述的日常生活影响人的心灵，为思考当今某些遭受歧视的社会群体提供了分析框架。读者如果对女权主义或者对文学批评感兴趣，这篇经典不容错过。

第一部分：学术渊源

1 作者生平与历史背景

要点 🔑

- 《一间自己的房间》在女权主义思想和社会运动史上是极为重要的文献，也是 20 世纪女性文学批评中最有影响力的一部作品。

- 伍尔芙的家教使她拥有了受教育的特权，但却仍无法与她的兄弟们所拥有的机会颉颃。

- 第一波女权主义初战告捷（19 世纪和 20 世纪初女权主义者的激进主义运动主要是争取法律上的平等），伍尔芙发现，在英国为女性争取平等的社会基本生活条件，与争取平等的法权一样重要。

为何要读这部著作？

《一间自己的房间》（1929）在女性主义思想史上是一部经典作品，弗吉尼亚·伍尔芙被认为是 20 世纪最重要的女性作家。该作品促使对于女性平等权益的讨论热度大涨，甚至超越了有关争取投票权等宪法法律权益的讨论。它探讨了日常生活状态对女性，尤其是对女性作家心理上的影响。

20 世纪初的女权主义论争大多是为女性争取一些主要的法律权益——特别是妇女选举权＊（在国家大选中的投票权）。而《一间自己的房间》关注日常生活对女性心理和才智的影响。该文试图回答一个问题：为什么文学正典＊（通常被认为是文学经典的那部分作品）中几乎看不到女性作家的作品。从文化唯物主义＊的视角进行考察发现，艺术与"物质"生活紧密关联——一个人的经济状况、衣着、占有私人空间的途径、与他人的交往——伍尔芙认为，受物质条件制约，从古至今许多女性作家具有创作潜能却无法施展，而男人却享有这些特权。伍尔芙质问道，历史上女作家既没有钱，又没有个人空间，还无法接受教育，如何指望她们从事文学创作？

《一间自己的房间》的出版对女权主义运动的转向具有催化作用。如今，该书学术内涵依然丰富，且引人深思。该书超越时代，提出的几个核心论题成为 20 世纪后半期女性主义者的主要议题，至今仍有影响力。要想深入解读伍尔芙及其作品，要想了解早期女权主义思想，必须阅读该书。它也是进行文学和女性主义研究的学生的必读篇目。

> "我刚冒雨从格顿*学院演讲回来，一群女生如饥似渴却意志坚定——给我留下的印象。还有就是，她们聪明，有理想，却很穷。她们注定会成为学校的女老师。"
>
> ——弗吉尼亚·伍尔芙：《作家日记》

作者生平

伍尔芙于 1882 年 1 月 25 日生于伦敦的肯辛顿区，是莱斯利·斯蒂芬*先生和朱莉亚·斯蒂芬夫妇的第三个孩子。伍尔芙的同胞兄弟姐妹有瓦内萨*（1879 年生），托比（1880 年生）和艾德恩（1883 年生）。伍尔芙的哥哥和弟弟一开始读寄宿学校，后来上了剑桥大学。女孩们则在家接受教育。不过，在父亲的书房里，她们能读到各种各样的书。弗吉尼亚就这样阅读了大量的英国文学和经典，为她成为作家打下了坚实的基础。

1904 年，父亲去世后，伍尔芙兄妹搬到了伦敦布卢姆斯伯里广场。在那里，她们和许多艺术家、文化人成了朋友，这个圈子后来成为有名的布卢姆斯伯里团体。该团体成员除了斯蒂芬兄妹，还有小说家 E.M. 福斯特 *、经济学家约翰·梅纳德·凯恩斯 * 和传记作家里顿·斯特拉奇 *。1912 年，弗吉尼亚与团体中成员伦纳德·伍尔夫 * 结婚，随夫姓伍尔芙，并以这个名字闻名。

1900 年，弗吉尼亚·伍尔芙以一名记者的身份开始了她的写作生涯。1907 年，她开始创作第一部小说。继小说《远航》（1915年出版）之后，她出版了 8 部小说，包括《达洛维夫人》（1925），《到灯塔去》（1927）和《海浪》（1931）。在她非小说类的著作中，最有名的是《现代小说》（1919）、《一间自己的房间》（1929）。这些著作在伍尔芙有生之年就使她成为了文学名人，如今，她更被公认为 20 世纪最伟大的作家之一。

在伍尔芙生活的时代，女性很难获得文学声誉或因智力超群受到尊敬。伍尔芙深知女性所面临的困难，深知天才女性生活在普遍歧视女性 *（仇恨女性）的社会里时心理上所承受的压力。伍尔芙一生承受着精神疾病和自杀冲动的折磨，最终在 1941 年完成了最后一部小说《幕间》后自杀。该书在她去世后出版。

创作背景

20 世纪 20 年代对英国、英国女性，以及各个门类的艺术而言都是一个关键时期。[1] 当时的大英帝国是世界上最强大的力量，一个拥有约 4 亿 5 千万人口的帝国——占世界总人口的 1/5——并在其统治区域内收获巨大的经济利益。[2] 科技发生了巨变，如收音机，激发了人们对于现代媒体各种可能性的畅想，这一切又深刻地影响了艺术以及日常生活。[3] 但与此同时，英国经历了第一次世界大战

（1914—1918）*，物质及人们的心理都遭受了巨大的损伤。

大约有 70 多万英国志愿军死亡——年龄段 19 至 22 岁差不多 35% 的男性——战争造成了社会的巨变，尤其是对女性而言。[4] 1918 年，30 岁以上的女性有了投票权。1928 年，在伍尔芙公开演讲《一间自己的房间》两个月前，议会通过了一项决议，即所有 21 岁以上的女性都拥有选举权。许多聆听伍尔芙 1928 年演讲的女大学生都属于新时代的女学生及新女性。这一时期英国女性走出家庭、在外工作的数量史无前例。

但是，即便如此，仍然有许多障碍阻挡着女性拥有一些权益。与男性相比，社会依旧不重视女性的价值，女性在物质上依旧没有很好的保障。如伍尔芙在访问剑桥大学时，该大学的女生没有正式学籍，这一状况直到 1948 年才得以解决。[5]

---

1 简明深入地了解伍尔芙的生平，请参阅米迦勒 H. 惠特沃思的《弗吉尼亚·伍尔芙》，牛津：牛津大学出版社，2005 年，第 2 章等处。

2 安格斯·麦迪逊：《世界经济：千年史》，巴黎：经济合作与发展组织，2001 年，第 98 页。

3 见塔潘·K. 萨卡等：《无线电史》，新泽西州霍博肯：交叉科学出版社，2006 年。

4 见约翰·基根：《第一次世界大战》，纽约：温特吉出版社，2000 年，第 439 页。

5 完整的历史请参阅丽塔·麦克威廉斯–托博格：《剑桥大学的女子：虽为混合型，却是男子大学》，伦敦：戈兰茨出版社，1975 年。

2 学术背景

要点 🔑

- 在父权 *（以男性为主导）社会里，女性的地位和生活过去是，现在仍然是女权主义思想和政治运动的核心。

- 早期女权主义运动主要为女性争取法律权益。1792 年，早期女权主义思想家玛丽·沃斯通克拉夫特 * 出版《女权辩》，首次提出女性身份低下一方面源于压制自由的社会惯习，另一方面源于女性缺乏受教育的机会。

- 与同时代的其他人不同，伍尔芙关注日常生活状态如何影响女性（特别是女性作家），并提出对女性而言拥有物质条件比获取法律权益更重要。

著作语境

弗吉尼亚·伍尔芙的《一间自己的房间》应该放到 3 个文化背景中去理解：伍尔芙生活的文化背景、女权主义发展史和文学史。

伍尔芙本人与当时的文学和思想界精英交往密切，从中获益不浅。她父亲莱斯利·斯蒂芬是一名记者、传记作家、思想史家，至今仍然以《英国人物传记词典》创始人身份而闻名于世。得益于斯蒂芬的博学，伍尔芙在丰富的文化环境里长大。其次，她的兄弟艾德恩和托比在剑桥大学 * 读书时，结交了几位天才思想家，并成为朋友。他们渐渐地都成为以思想家和艺术家为主的布卢姆斯伯里团体的核心成员。经两个兄弟的引荐，伍尔芙结识了这些思想界精英。

当时，女权主义运动的思想正在开始改变。为女性争取更多的权益，不断遭遇到社会旧俗偏见的坚决抗拒。而且，女权主义团体内部在女性本质的问题上也存在激烈争论。英语文学专家米迦勒·惠特沃思指出，1918 年妇女刚刚获得部分选举权，就即刻分裂成"旧""新"女权主义两个阵营。[1] 前者认为，妇女作为人（从根本上与男性一样）应该拥有完全平等的权利。后者在追求男女平等的同时也强调性别差异。这一论争与伍尔芙在《一间自己的房间》里提出的精神"雌雄同体"*一致——人的精神既非男性也非女性，或既是男性也是女性。[2]

最后，现代主义运动*于 20 世纪初发轫，并持续了几十年。某些领域如建筑和音乐一开始强调打破传统，接着又强调重建传统。1918 年后的 10 年中，英语文学取得了巨大成就：詹姆斯·乔伊斯*的小说《尤利西斯》（1918 年以连载的形式发表，1922 年出版单行本）、T.S. 艾略特*的长诗《荒原》（1922）、诗人与小说家 D.H. 劳伦斯*的《查特莱夫人的情人》（1928）都是现代主义里程碑式的作品。现代主义运动的最核心要素，正如艾略特在其最重要的论文《传统与个人才能》（1919）中所论述的，是其与传统、与文学正典之间的关系。这对伍尔芙在《一间自己的房间》中思考女性正典的可能性至关重要。[3]

> "你是否注意到一年中有几本书是写女性的？你是否注意到其中有几本是男性作家写的呢？你是否发现，或许，你就是这个宇宙中被谈论得最多的动物？"
>
> ——弗吉尼亚·伍尔芙：《一间自己的房间》

学科概览

《一间自己的房间》同时分属3个学术领域：它是一篇女性主义者的辩词（该说法颇有争议），是一篇文学理论文本，也是一部小说。它吸收也回应了上述3个领域对其的影响。

女权主义——常常指"妇女问题"——是20世纪初期英国争论的焦点话题，伍尔芙在思考女作家在世界上的地位时参考了许多先例。在《女权辩》（1792）中，女权主义先锋玛丽·沃斯通克拉夫特指出，教育的缺失阻碍了女性成为一名（与男性）平等的社会人。[4] 美国女权主义者玛格丽特·福勒*1843年撰写了著名的《19世纪妇女》，也曾极力呼吁给予女性接受教育的权利和谋求职业的机会。伍尔芙追随两位前辈的步伐，考察了女性经济状况和文学创造力之间的关系。

《一间自己的房间》在文学理论和小说发展史上也有先例可循。把现代主义的魔幻与过去的文学惯例——"传统"结合起来，T.S.艾略特的"传统与个人才能"功不可没。艾略特认为，作家要创作，首先要对伟大的前辈作家有深刻理解，这一思想自20世纪30年代开始，成为英美文学批评界的主流。伍尔芙顺应潮流，提出女性作家需要有自己的"前辈范例"。《一间自己的房间》在形式和风格上也体现了诸多现代主义元素：论述与小说两种文体的杂合，文本专注于叙述者的意识和感知。这是典型的现代主义叙事，也是伍尔芙小说的典型叙事方式。

学术渊源

《一间自己的房间》受到哪位早期女权主义作家的直接影响，

14

尽管难寻其迹，但该书无疑受到了当时女权主义思想的影响。牛津大学学者索文·帕克曾记述道，伍尔芙在文本中随处可见的论述得益于诸如英国演员和女性主义者西塞莉·汉密尔顿*、美国作家夏洛特·帕金斯·吉尔曼*等。[5] 在伍尔芙虚构朱迪斯·莎士比亚（虚构的威廉·莎士比亚*的妹妹）之前，汉密尔顿于1909年在其创作的《婚姻如交易》中已经辨析过为什么没有出现与莎士比亚旗鼓相当的女作家。[6] 同时，吉尔曼则在她的《男人制作的世界：或我们的大男子主义文化》（1911）中，抨击了男人征服女性造成的心理影响。[7]

广义地说，伍尔芙所受的影响，来自于布卢姆斯伯里团体成员，以及与她交往过的艺术家们。伍尔芙在撰写评论，经营霍加斯出版社*（由伍尔芙和她丈夫经营）出书业务时，以及个人交往中，邂逅了T.S.艾略特和詹姆斯·乔伊斯的作品。布卢姆斯伯里团体本身就是一个大熔炉，各种激进的思想在这里碰撞，各种艺术、思想和性别的试验在这里进行着——所有这些都反映在《一间自己的房间》中。团体成员如经济学家约翰·梅纳德·凯恩斯、传记作家里顿·斯特拉奇、批评家克莱夫·贝尔*、画家罗杰·弗莱*在各自领域中都是激进运动的急先锋。他们质疑当时流行的观念，他们对伍尔芙的影响在她的著作里无处不在，《一间自己的房间》犹甚。[8]

---

1 米迦勒·惠特沃思：《弗吉尼亚·伍尔芙》，牛津：牛津大学出版社，2005年，第62页。

2 弗吉尼亚·伍尔芙：《一间自己的房间》和《三枚旧金币》，安娜·斯奈思编，牛津：牛津大学出版社，2015年，第74页。

3　T.S.艾略特："传统与个人才能"，载《艾略特论文选》，伦敦：费伯兄弟出版社，1951年。

4　见玛丽·沃斯通克拉夫特：《女权辩》，黛德丽·肖纳·林奇编，纽约：W.W.诺顿出版社，2009年。

5　索文·S.帕克："父权制与弗吉尼亚·伍尔芙：单声背后的众生"，《英语研究评论》第56卷，2005年第223期，第122页。

6　西塞莉·汉密尔顿：《婚姻如交易》，纽约：莫弗特亚德出版社，1909年，第14—16章。

7　夏洛特·帕金斯·吉尔曼：《男人制作的世界：或我们的大男子主义文化》，纽约：查尔顿出版社，1911年。

8　布卢姆斯伯里团体的参考文献有：弗朗西斯·斯伯丁：《布卢姆斯伯里团体》，伦敦：国家肖像美术馆，2005年；雷·格兰特·罗宾斯：《布卢姆斯伯里团体：文献节选》第一版，华盛顿州肯莫尔：价格指南出版社，1978年；海因茨·安托尔：《布卢姆斯伯里团体：哲学、美学和文学成就》，海德堡：C.温特，1986年。

3 主导命题

要点 🔑

- 弗吉尼亚·伍尔芙的作品探讨了两个中心论题：为什么文学正典里鲜有女性作家？女性作家创作出伟大的小说必须具备哪些条件？

- 当伍尔芙创作的时候，历史上缺少女性作家和艺术家常被作为证明女性智力低下的论据。

- 伍尔芙考察了历史上的社会与物质条件如何让女性作家失声，从而挑战了该设想。

核心问题

　　弗吉尼亚·伍尔芙的《一间自己的房间》原书名是《女人与小说》，但如同伍尔芙开篇所言，文章故意没有回答"女性的本质和小说的本质这样重大的问题"。[1] 取而代之，伍尔芙提出了两个核心问题：为什么文学正典鲜有女性作家？女性作家要创作伟大的小说必须具备哪些条件？

　　第一个问题直击当时大量反女权主义者言辞的要害：女性在智力和能力上都比男性弱。从古至今，著名女作家和女艺术家的缺失常被当作上述假设的依据。但伍尔芙认为，智力和才华没有性别的差异，是平等的，并且进而质疑是什么样的历史条件妨碍了女性成为伟大的作家。为了反驳女性缺少文学创作才能的谬论，她还探寻了女性写作传统匮乏的根源。

　　第二个核心问题与当时英国如火如荼的妇女运动*（常用该术

语指称女性争取选举权和早期女权运动）有关。虽然妇女在 1928 年获得了全部的选举权，两个月之后伍尔芙发表数场后来名为《一间自己的房间》的演讲，但当时女性依然承受着偏见。社会期望（诸如教育、婚姻和工作）、沿袭已久的法规条例（如女学生在剑桥大学直到 1948 年才有资格获取学位）和物质条件（缺少金钱和私人空间）仍然使英国女性低人一等。伍尔芙质问道，社会必须改变什么才能让女性创作出比肩历史上男性作家的伟大作品？

> "我想过被人关在门外是多么不快；转念一想被人锁在门里可能更糟。我想到一种性别享受着安全和财产，而另一种性别遭遇着贫穷和不安，以及拥有或缺失传统对作家思想会有什么影响。最终，我认为该丢掉一天来的烦心事。"
>
> ——弗吉尼亚·伍尔芙：《一间自己的房间》

参与者

在伍尔芙时代，"女性问题"是炙手可热的争议焦点。即使女性的法律权益有所增加，社会陋习却依然未改。1911 年，南非小说家、女权主义者奥莉芙·施莱纳 * 在《女性与劳工》中指出，女性被"绑住了手和脚……被人为制定的规矩，也被陋习绑住了，这些都是旧社会的残余"。[2] 一战 * 虽然给女性创造了较多的机会（也制造了各种需求），让她们走出家庭，加入到社会工作中，并超越了传统角色，但这一进步遭到了反女权主义者，甚至厌女者——"憎恨妇女"——的激烈反应。

在《一间自己的房间》中，伍尔芙以漫画笔法虚构了"冯·X

教授"来再现这一激烈反应，他写了一部"里程碑式著作"，名为《低能的女性性别：智力、道德、身体》。[3] 现实中反女权主义者的极端程度与伍尔芙文中的教授相比，有过之而无不及。在 19 世纪后半叶，哈佛大学医科教授爱德华·克拉克*曾提出，对女性进行"男性化"的教育会摧毁女性的身体。[4] 在伍尔芙生活的年代，奥地利哲学家奥托·魏宁格*在《性与性格》（1903）中写到，人的性格是两种气质，即男性和女性气质的混合体，而女性气质则仅是消极品质的根源所在。[5]

这场争论的另一方则是女权主义的急先锋，代表人物有奥莉芙·施莱纳、伊丽莎白·罗宾斯*、埃莉诺·拉斯伯恩*和雷·斯特拉奇*。[6] 她们与一些团体如英国第一个为妇女赢得国家层面选举权的妇女组织"伦敦女性选举权社团"联合，既为妇女获取全部的选举权，也为拓展女性主义观点而积极地努力着。

当代论战

女性权益论争以广为流传的假设为中心，即女性要么比男性低能，要么因"天生"在某些方面与男性不同，因此只适合做某些事情，有些事情她们则被排除在外。克拉克的《教育中的性》（1873）就是后者的范例。克拉克在文中从病理学和医药学方面为"女性气质"制定了检测标准，也就是说，从诊断医学角度分析了女性气质。这一检验标准在 20 世纪 20 年代依然很有权威性。克拉克陈述说，"男性不比女性优越，女性也不比男性优越"，但是，男女"天然"有别，这一点不容忽视。[7] 比如"让女孩去男孩（学校）生活"，其结果是"女孩的身体系统会出现紊乱"。所以克拉克说，"在上帝和人类面前，一视同仁地教育性别不同的男女是有罪的。"[8]

奥托·魏宁格则毫不掩饰对女性的憎恶:"女性要素"都是负面的,女性身上哪怕一点点优良的品质都是"男性"特征。"所有著名的以及智力超群的女性",他写道,都拥有"一些解剖学的男性特征"。男性特征成就了她们,这些品质令人印象深刻。[9]论及女性和艺术,他同样非常直接地指出,"从没有女性天才……以后也不会有"。[10]这种术语"(女性天才)自相矛盾,因为天才只不过是强化的,……普遍意识的男性。"[11]

女权运动本身就是女性权力和能力大讨论的营地。如同施莱纳所说,人们普遍认为,社会现状和排外主义不知不觉地把女性推进"寄生"(依靠男人)的状态中。女性被剥夺了参加各种形式积极且有意识的社会劳动的权利,从而(降格)到只能被动地参加一些仅属于发挥女性性别功能的活动,最终成为"弱势性别"。[12]

---

1 弗吉尼亚·伍尔芙:《一间自己的房间》和《三枚旧金币》,安娜·斯奈思编,牛津:牛津大学出版社,2015年,第4页。

2 奥莉芙·施莱纳:《女性与劳工》,伦敦:T.费希尔·昂温出版社,1911年,第24页。

3 伍尔芙:《一间自己的房间》,第24页。

4 见爱德华·H.克拉克:《教育中的性:女孩的公平机会》(1873),载南希·F.科特编,《痛苦的根源:美国妇女社会史文献》,新罕布什尔州黎巴嫩:新英格兰大学出版社,1996年,第331页。

5 见奥托·魏宁格:《性与性格》,伦敦:威廉·海涅曼出版社,1906年。

6 索文·S.帕克:"选举权与弗吉尼亚·伍尔芙:'单声背后的众生'",《英语研究评论》第56卷,2005年第223期,第122—123页。

7　克拉克：《教育中的性》，第 330 页。

8　克拉克：《教育中的性》，第 331 页。

9　魏宁格：《性与性格》，第 65 页。

10　魏宁格：《性与性格》，第 189 页。

11　魏宁格：《性与性格》，第 189 页。

12　施莱纳：《妇女与劳工》，第 78 页。

4 作者贡献

要点 🔑

- 弗吉尼亚·伍尔芙提出,女性要创作出伟大的文学作品,需保障她们有稳定的收入和属于自己的私人空间。

- 伍尔芙提出,物质保障对女性进行文学创作至关重要,由此可以认为,女性并非本质上就比男性缺少创作伟大作品的能力,而是受条件的限制。

- 伍尔芙的观点,在当时主要的女权主义运动中都已论及,但她的阐述方法十分独特。

作者目标

弗吉尼亚·伍尔芙的《一间自己的房间》脱胎于她 1928 年 10 月分别在纽汉姆学院 * 和格顿学院 * 做的两场讲座。这两所女子学院当时属于剑桥大学。结束了格顿学院演讲,从剑桥大学返回后,伍尔芙在日记中写道,她"直白地告诉女孩子们去喝红酒,要一间属于自己的屋子"——一则陈旧且戏谑的评论,实际上直击伍尔芙演讲的核心:女性只有取得与男性平等的物质条件后才能写出伟大的作品。[1] 也就是说,女性争取的全面法律平等权益(如投票权和工作权),之前从未被赋予,虽然得了一些进展,但她们的物质条件依旧不如男性。与男性比较,她们普遍收入少,生活更艰辛,私人空间狭窄。

伍尔芙意指物质上的不平等普遍给女性,尤其是女作家带来困扰。在《一间自己的房间》最后一篇文章中,伍尔芙从 4 个方面进行论述：探讨为什么过去鲜有女性作家；探讨女作家缺失的传统对当今女作家的影响；无论是字面含义还是隐喻含义，女性都被各种理由或关进了某些空间里（例如家里），或挡在了某些空间外（例如某些只有男性的机构）；探讨基本生活条件如何影响人的意识和能力。

尽管伍尔芙的上述想法多数在当时已经很流行，但她从文学创作角度关注物质条件对女性创作的影响，其视角非常独特。正如英国文学专家劳拉·马库斯所评论的，《一间自己的房间》可能依然是"20 世纪女权主义批评理论的最好典范"。[2]

> "或许你们会问，我们请你来谈谈女性和小说——这与一间自己的房间有何干系？我接下来尽量解释清楚。"
>
> ——弗吉尼亚·伍尔芙：《一间自己的房间》

研究方法

虽然这本书脱胎于一系列讲座，《一间自己的房间》还是论文和短篇小说的混合体。文本一开始就用了一个中间句（"但，你可能会问"），仿佛读者走进演讲室时已经迟到了。讲述者继续说，她打算好好利用"小说家被赋予的全部自由和特权"来阐释她的主题。接下来，伍尔芙以小说家的笔法，描述她在剑桥（在一所男子学院和一所女子学院用餐）和伦敦（为讲座做准备，读一本当代女作家的小说）的经历，附带进行思想实验，叙述人想象着伊丽莎白*（英国伊丽莎白女王一世，她统治的时间是 1558 到 1603 年）时代的英国天才女性可能会过的生活。

伍尔芙创造了一种独特的研究方法，那就是把女性作家和关于她们在历史上地位的文艺批评，以及以作家身份描写自己作为女性的经历的一手资料进行整合。这使她把传统文学批评的分析逻辑和历史证据，与叙述小说的情感资源有机结合起来。伍尔芙的研究途径还意味着，她可以对"女性问题"做出贡献，她可以批判性地调查"女性问题"。这迥异于如奥莉芙·施莱纳等作家采用的热情洋溢的政治辩论模式。通过讲述和理解她的论点，伍尔芙鼓励读者与叙述者达成一致。

伍尔芙研究女性问题的另一个关键要素在于她关注生活的物质条件。叙述者陈述说，有钱比有投票权"似乎更加重要"，这一说法一直存在争议。[3]然而，它强调的是伍尔芙的文化物质主义信仰——设想人的能力与其经济状况，甚至与生活中最细微的物质条件密切相关。

时代贡献

正如劳拉·马库斯所评价的，《一间自己的房间》关注的是人而不是政治事件，因此已经成为了20世纪后半期女权主义者和女性主义文学批评的重要作品。[4]然而，索文·帕克和亚历克斯·兹沃德林两位学者却认为，尽管《一间自己的房间》有很多创新，但文中伍尔芙论及的见解毕竟在当时女权主义者的写作中已经被讨论过。

兹沃德林指出，伍尔芙有意识地模仿一个多世纪前由玛丽·沃斯通克拉夫特撰写《女权辩》时创造的文学传统，这一传统影响了伍尔芙的少年、青年，甚至整个成年。[5]然而，他同时指出，"伍尔芙对女权主义遗产的态度主要是修正主义的。"[6]伍尔芙青年时期参与的妇女争取选举权运动就是比较典型的例子，当时几乎只是关注

女性的选举权益，相信只要拥有了选举权，女性期待的其他改变就
会随之发生。伍尔芙对此公开表示怀疑，相信"心灵要比法律难以
改变"。也就是说，只有社会态度和物质状况允许男人和女人在思
想上承认双方是平等的，才会带来真正的改变。

　　尽管从法律方面来说，女性的自由尚待继续努力，但女性在
1928 年就赢得了主要的权益。而伍尔芙的研究兴趣主要在于导致
男性继续主导社会的心理和经济原因。《一间自己的房间》把女权
主义者关注的焦点折回到更加宽泛、更加复杂的问题上，而非仅仅
是法律权益。这一转变应该视作既属于女权主义传统，也是当时语
境中新的创造。

1　弗吉尼亚·伍尔芙:《作家日记》，伦纳德·伍尔夫编，伦敦:哈考特出版社，
　　1954 年，第 134 页。

2　劳拉·马库斯:《弗吉尼亚·伍尔芙》第 2 版，塔维斯托克:诺思科特出版社，
　　2004 年，第 43 页。

3　弗吉尼亚·伍尔芙:《一间自己的房间》和《三枚旧金币》，安娜·斯奈思编，
　　牛津:牛津大学出版社，2015 年，第 29 页。

4　马库斯:《弗吉尼亚·伍尔芙》，第 41 页。

5　亚历克斯·兹沃德林:《弗吉尼亚·伍尔芙与真实的世界》，柏克利:加州大学
　　出版社，1986 年，第 211 页。

6　兹沃德林:《伍尔芙与真实的世界》，第 211 页。

第二部分：学术思想

5 思想主脉

要点 🔑

- 《一间自己的房间》的核心主题是，从古至今父权（男性主导）社会为女性设置了经济和物质方面的阻碍，从而制约了女性潜能的发挥。

- 弗吉尼亚·伍尔芙认为，女性创作小说——进入文学正典行列——必须有稳定的收入，并且有自己的空间。

- 伍尔芙通过以小说的笔法描述 20 世纪初她本人作为女性的亲身经历，以及考察 16 世纪以来女性的生活和作品来阐释她的观点。

核心主题

正如伍尔芙所言，《一间自己的房间》的核心主题是"物质是思想自由的保障"。[1] 她用让人过目不忘的简洁文字总结了上述观点，并用来命名书中一篇论文，即"女人要写小说，必须先有钱，有一间自己的房间"。[2] 她还列举了钱的具体数额，即年收入 500 英镑——相当于今天的 28 000 多英镑（超过 43 000 美元）。[3]

伍尔芙提出的要求，既是实际所需，也有深意：就她个人而言，这是实际需求，但也代表了更深远的意义。钱"代表着有权去深思熟虑，……门上的锁意味着有权为自己思考。"[4] 她的主要论点是：思考能力的提高，更确切地说，写作的才华，靠的不是天才先天具备的浪漫情怀，而是最基本的生活条件：人生存所需的食物、衣服、能活动或者静思的空间，以及社会规约所允许或者期待你的行为方式。

这一观点背后隐藏着伍尔芙颇具争议的思想，即钱和个人空间比女人获得投票权更重要。为了证明这一点，伍尔芙引用当代文学批评家亚瑟·奎勒·库奇*的话，"我们可能胡诌些民主之类的东西，但实际上，英国的穷孩子和雅典奴隶的儿子一样，思想被解放的希望渺茫，而伟大作品往往诞生于思想自由之中。"[5]她说，当代女性就像奎勒·库奇笔下的穷孩子："女性自古生来就穷，……比雅典奴隶的儿子所拥有的思想自由还要少。"[6]甚至就投票权而言，不改善经济和物质环境，就无法达成真正的"思想解放"。

> "（这些）创作并非子虚乌有，凭空捏造，而是靠实实在在的人创造出来的。而人则与物质基础相关，如健康、钱和居住的房屋。"
>
> ——弗吉尼亚·伍尔芙：《一间自己的房间》

思想探究

在《一间自己的房间》中，伍尔芙的论述集中在文化物质主义上。文化物质主义认为，个人的性格、智力和信仰的形成受社会结构和经济条件的制约。也就是说，社会文化——从流行歌曲到报纸、艺术、诗歌和小说——受其社会的生活"物质条件"所影响：个体收入的多少，所受到教育的途径，负担得起的住房，买得起的食物。这与当时流行的观点完全相反，即认为"艺术"完全是个人能力的产物，就像伍尔芙所言，他们的思想已"超越这些物质的东西"。[7]伍尔芙认为，如果相信有可能做到"艺术超越物质"，那就忽略了日常生活对艺术家的影响。

除"文化物质主义"之外，伍尔芙另一个主要观点是伟大的艺术是从传统中衍生的。这也是现代主义 * 文学运动的核心命题。该命题由伍尔芙同时代的庞德 * 和 T.S. 艾略特口头提出，书面表达出现在影射文学的作品中，如乔伊斯 * 的著名小说《尤利西斯》。用伍尔芙的话说，"杰作的诞生不会是孤零零地横空出世，一般情况下，一定是多年思考的结晶，而且是多人思考的结晶，因此，单人发声的背后一定隐藏着众多人的经历"。[8] 换句话说，作家都在继承前辈。

这些思想综合阐释了历史上女性作家缺失的原因。首先，男性主导的社会——标准的女权主义术语就是"父权制"——导致女性一直无法获取经济独立和写作所需要的私人空间。其次，这导致了为数不多的天才女性缺乏物质条件，无法书写女性文学传统，而文学传统则是当代女性创造伟大文学的必要条件。历史上鲜有伟大的女性作家，这并非女性不能创作的证据，只能证明女性由于受到社会条件的制约，被迫不能写作。

语言表述

《一间自己的房间》不只容易读懂，而且作品形式引人入胜。它融合了批评写作、演讲技巧和小说——著名的伍尔芙式叙述技法。虽然文中以第一人称叙事，叙述人说话时常用"我"，但伍尔芙澄清说，"我"不是指作者她本人，"这是我（叫我玛丽·波顿、玛丽·斯通、玛丽·卡尔麦克或随便什么，都无关紧要）"。[9] 伍尔芙用这种方式指出，与前辈们比较，20 世纪 20 年代女性的生活境况没得到改善，男权社会虽然口头承认她们是独立的个体，但对待她们的方式在很多方面与前辈女性遭遇的一样。这是伍尔芙女性观的主旨。在伍尔芙的文中有 3 个人，出自 16 世纪一个芭蕾舞剧，分别是叙述人的姊姊、虚构的 "Ferham" 学院的院长和女作家。通过这一策略，她把许多真实生活中的要素和女性经历进行合成，生动地展现在读者面前。虽然是真实的第一手材料，但通过叙述人虚构的经历进行表现。

《一间自己的房间》除了形式上的创造——这一创造性手法也表现在伍尔芙的小说中，还用了许多幽默与反讽的手法，其使用频率不亚于对主题作直接的批评分析。伍尔芙的叙述者公开嘲笑男性"权威"，他们创作"厌女"文学，好像这就是科学事实。

她描述了一幅被切割的 "X 教授" 肖像，想象着"一个男人吸引着无数女人，……他有着肥大的下颌垂肉，一双小眼睛，面庞很红。但这幅肖像不是出现在我的图像中"[10]另外，写到"那些伟大的男人"，他们从古至今（尽管女性地位显然低人一等）都爱着女人。叙述人反讽地指出，"所有这些关系都是柏拉图式的［即，没有性］，我却不会承认。"[11]类似尖刻的冷笑话贯穿文本始终。

1　弗吉尼亚·伍尔芙：《一间自己的房间》和《三枚旧金币》，安娜·斯奈思编，牛津：牛津大学出版社，2015 年，第 81 页。

2　伍尔芙：《一间自己的房间》，第 3 页。

3　根据英国银行的通货膨胀计算器：http://www.bankofengland.co.uk/education/Pages/resources/inflationtools/caculator/flash/default.aspx，登录日期 2015 年 8 月 5 日。

4　伍尔芙：《一间自己的房间》，第 80 页。

5　伍尔芙:《一间自己的房间》，第81页，转引自亚瑟·奎勒-库奇:《论写作的艺术》，纽约：G.P.普特南森出版社，1916年，第39页。

6　伍尔芙:《一间自己的房间》，第81页。

7　伍尔芙:《一间自己的房间》，第81页。

8　伍尔芙:《一间自己的房间》，第49页。

9　伍尔芙:《一间自己的房间》，第4页。

10　伍尔芙:《一间自己的房间》，第24页。

11　伍尔芙:《一间自己的房间》，第65页。

6 思想支脉

要点 ⚷

- 《一间自己的房间》中有两个次要观点，但很重要。第一，想象或揭开被隐藏的女性文学正典是有可能的；其次，写作与性别的关系密切且复杂。

- 上述第一点强化了历史上女性受到种种条件限制无法创作的观点；第二点使伍尔芙提出如下问题：女性文学正典将是或该是什么样的。

- 事实证明，非传统的女性文学史对随后的女权主义文学批评影响极大。

其他思想

伍尔芙《一间自己的房间》影响力最大的一点是有关虚构人物"朱迪思·莎士比亚"的思想实验。通过虚构的威廉·莎士比亚的妹妹朱迪思，伍尔芙指明历史上人们用种种办法让女性保持沉默，或者压制女性发声。正如伍尔芙所言，这种压制既不是那么简单为之，也不是故意之举。这一行为复杂且间接：朱迪思的父亲因为爱她，不想让她因不被社会接纳而痛苦，所以不鼓励她阅读。[1] 像哥哥一样，朱迪思为了追求创作和表演的梦想逃到了伦敦。但是，威廉在伦敦受到了欢迎，而她则被嘲笑，被排斥，最后非法怀孕并自杀。[2] 伍尔芙用这一想象的生活，回答了历史上如何以及为何缺乏女作家的范例的问题。

从"朱迪思·莎士比亚"切换成伍尔芙的叙述人，伍尔芙借其叙述人罗列了英国历史上为数不多的几位女性作家：阿芙拉·贝恩*，勃朗特＊三姐妹，简·奥斯汀＊，乔治·艾略特＊，她们构成了英国文学中稀松的"女性传统"。叙述人最初认为，女作家的"创造力""与男作家的创造力相比有很大的不同"，女作家在创作中应该反映这样的不同。[3] 然而，接下来叙述人反问自己，写作是否该这样划分性别？如果有"智力的两性对应着身体的两性"，"那么为了获取彻底的满足和最大的幸福，作家能否让两性联合起来"，以创作出伟大的文学？[4] 果真如此，这样的结合会否扰乱"女性写作"或者有可能写出"女性文学正典"的想法？

> "我想象莎士比亚有一个才华出众的妹妹，名叫朱迪思，我们说……她跟哥哥一样大胆、富有想象力，一样对探索世界充满好奇。但是，她从未进过学校。"
>
> ——弗吉尼亚·伍尔芙：《一间自己的房间》

思想探究

在《一间自己的房间》里，女性声音遭到压制的观点主要通过朱迪思展现。伍尔芙通过创造与历史上英国最伟大的男性作家相对应的女性人物来说明莎士比亚时代的女性无论天赋如何都不可能成为"莎士比亚"。虚构人物"朱迪思"也说明压制女性具有方法多样、手段间接等特征：不是有意让她们沉默，也不是因为男性痛恨女性，而是社会状况就是如此。她"是父亲的掌上明珠"，"尼克·格林尼……同情她"；她生命中的男人善待她，但是目的是让朱迪思变得顺从和安静。[5] 伍尔芙继而说道，让一个 16 世纪的妇女具备"莎士比亚的天才"是不可能的，因为天才"不会在贫苦、没有受过教育、缺乏独立的人中产生"，而当时女性的状况正是这样。[6]

《一间自己的房间》抨击了厌女症人群——在 X 教授仇恨的背后是"伪装起来的愤怒和其他复杂的因素",如朱迪思遭受到的压制,强调了男性主导的社会对女性普遍存在着无意识即非有意的征服性。在其他文本里,伍尔芙借刻画一个颇具反讽却又不失礼貌的人物形象表达了同样的观点。这个人不让叙述人进入她访问的男子学院的图书馆,他是"守护的天使","满头银发的善良绅士,凡事不以为然"。女性如果没有本院同事作陪或者没有介绍信,不许进入图书馆。他为此感到遗憾。[7]

这一见解促使伍尔芙想象,女性在"无休止的不被人看见的生活"中丢失了什么?想象历史上男性声音下面有一股被迫沉默的声音。[8] 这是该文本能持续对女权主义文学批评做出贡献的观点,即伍尔芙请读者想象被那种沉默欺骗的可能性:"当……一个人读到女巫被沉入水中,或者读到一位妇女生活在恶魔的魔掌下,读到一位聪明的妇女卖草药……那么,我想我们正在追踪迷失的小说家、被压制的诗人、某个沉默而不够光彩的简·奥斯丁。"[9] 对伍尔芙而言,这沉默仍然预示着这样一个问题,即真正的"女性小说"将是像什么样子——这个问题直接导出了文本中没有充分展开讨论的一个观点:文学的雌雄同体。

被忽视之处

《一间自己的房间》文本简短,影响巨大。本书篇幅有限,很难在此论述伍尔芙在书中未论及的思想。但是,叙述人对写作是否能够或者应该"性别化"(即男性或者女性)表达模糊,不如文本的中心意思清晰明了。人们在讨论该文本时也常常将此忽略。重要的是，读者常常把《一间自己的房间》当作一部同性恋文本，把《一间自己的房间》认作是最早的"酷儿"*文本（即最近被称为在异性恋之外的一种对身份考察的文化和理论潮流的文本）和女权主义文本。

在第五章里，叙述人提出"女性小说"只能从女性文学传统中产出，因为女性的"创造力大大地不同"于男性。[10] 后来，她质疑了这一提法。她看到一对夫妇一起坐进伦敦出租车，这一举动使她产生一个疑惑："人的大脑里是否有两种性别意识"，如同身体一样。男女在文学作品里是否该像生活中一样，为了实现"完全的满意和幸福"，他们必须达成平衡。[11] 如果这一认识成立的话，那是否存在"女性"写作？或者所有作家应该都是"雌雄同体"——同时既是男性也是女性？

思想上持"男人女性化"或者"女人男性化"，人是"女性""男性"性别同时共有的想法，已经是当代性别理论中的常见主题——包括著名的澳大利亚哲学家奥托·魏宁格的厌恶女性的著作《性与性格》。伍尔芙非常熟悉这部著作。[12] "双性同体"常常与同性恋有关——正如魏宁格推测，古典女同性恋诗人萨福*（大约公元前 630—公元前 570 年）的男性特征多于女性。[13] 伍尔芙清楚地知道，读者可能认为《一间自己的房间》潜含着女同性恋的主题，因此，在该文本出版前她在日记里写道，她会因此被"暗示为萨福主义者"（一位女同性恋）。[14] 尽管时至今日，评论界依然认为仅仅只是文中有此暗指，但女同性恋主义的确是伍尔芙个人性倾向的一个重要方面。她写于 1928 年的长篇小说《奥兰多》，就是描写一个人因不堪长期忍受着性别倒错的生活而变了性。劳拉·马库斯指出，《奥兰多》是对她当时的情人薇塔·萨克维尔·韦斯特*的一封"公开的情书"。[15] 诸如此类，可作一简单总结：文学"双性同体"不仅对"女性写作"，而且对即将众人皆知的"酷儿写作"而言，都是一个非常重要的概念。

---

1 弗吉尼亚·伍尔芙：《一间自己的房间》和《三枚旧金币》，安娜·斯奈思编，牛津：牛津大学出版社，2015年，第36页。

2 伍尔芙：《一间自己的房间》，第36—37页。

3 伍尔芙：《一间自己的房间》，第66页。

4 伍尔芙：《一间自己的房间》，第74页。

5 伍尔芙：《一间自己的房间》，第36、37页。

6 伍尔芙：《一间自己的房间》，第37页。

7 伍尔芙：《一间自己的房间》，第6页。

8 伍尔芙：《一间自己的房间》，第67页。

9 伍尔芙：《一间自己的房间》，第37页。

10 伍尔芙：《一间自己的房间》，第66页。

11 伍尔芙：《一间自己的房间》，第74页。

12 奥托·魏宁格：《性与性格》，伦敦：威廉·海涅曼出版社，1906年。

13 奥托·魏宁格：《性与性格》，第66页。

14 弗吉尼亚·伍尔芙：《作家日记》，伦纳德·伍尔夫编，伦敦：哈考特出版社，1954年，第148页。

15 劳拉·马库斯：《弗吉尼亚·伍尔芙》第2版，塔维斯托克：诺思科特出版社，2004年，第55页。

7 历史成就

要点 ⚷━

- 弗吉尼亚·伍尔芙的《一间自己的房间》受到当代读者的热烈欢迎，已经连续影响了好几代女权主义者。

- 伍尔芙小说创作的成功帮助《一间自己的房间》扩大了读者群，由此，伍尔芙观点可信度也得到了充分的证明。

- 《一间自己的房间》至今影响力不减，文本在其他语境中可利用的潜力尚有待开发，但也有其局限性，即文本中的论点仅针对20世纪20年代的英国。

观点评价

在早期评论弗吉尼亚·伍尔芙《一间自己的房间》的批评家中，批评家兼小说家阿诺德·贝内特*很快就注意到，该书的中心"论点"实际上十分简单——一个人若想写小说或诗歌，一年至少有500镑的收入和一间能上锁的房间。贝内特认为，这个观点"不可靠"。[1] 在贝内特看来，俄罗斯的伟大作家费奥多尔·陀思妥耶夫斯基和他本人就是例证，足以证明他的上述观点。然而，贝内特的评论事实上忽略了伍尔芙观点所指涉的一个更大的主旨——"思想的解放离不开物质条件"，历史上女性在物质条件上远不如男性。[2] 她通过生动的描述，让读者感受到，恶劣的物质条件不仅在过去给人的身心造成了影响，还借叙述人之口说出恶劣的物质条件给她同时代人的身心也造成了影响。由此，在伍尔芙看起来肤浅的论述背后，《一间自己的房间》提供了说服力很强的论据。

　　然而，除了上述观点，在其他方面很难定位《一间自己的房间》。贝内特毫不留情地指出，《一间自己的房间》学科定位不清晰，满篇都是"陈词赘句"，因为伍尔芙"无所不谈，偏偏不论及文本的主旨"。[3] 在某种意义上这确实是实情：伍尔芙为该领域拓展了可供考察的方方面面，为"女性与小说"话题提供了好几个观察视角，却故意回避结论的清晰性。然而，这是该文本研究模式的关键所在，也是考察复杂问题的关键所在。在开放性的段落中——叙述人登场之前——伍尔芙暗示地指出，钱和房间在文本里属于"次要的部分"；[4] 又通过暗示指出，文本的核心是"尚未解决的问题"——"女性的本质和小说的本质"。[5] 对这些话题依然保持着开放式结尾是该文本的关键所在，也是该文本里的观点至今对读者具有启发的原因所在。

> "（当）我请求你写更多的书时，我是在催促你做一件对你自己，对这个世界都好的事情。"
>
> ——弗吉尼亚·伍尔芙：《一间自己的房间》

当时的成就

　　1929 年《一间自己的房间》发表时，尽管伍尔芙在文学创作上已经获得了成功，该文本还是助她成为当时一颗最璀璨的文学明星。从 1925 年起，她发表了 3 部小说：《达洛维夫人》（1925）、《到灯塔去》（1927）和《奥兰多》（1928），奠定了她成为英国最重要小说家之一的地位。1927 年，她靠写小说赚取的年收入刚超过 500 镑。小说《奥兰多》出版后，她写书赚取的收入是原来的 3 倍。[6]《一间自己的房间》出版后，评论界赞扬声一片，因此，此书的销售速度超过了她之前所有的书。[7]在英格兰，霍加斯出版社（由伍尔芙和她丈夫伦纳德一起经营）在初版后的6个月里印刷了14 650本。[8]

《一间自己的房间》至今依然是一部重要文本，它不仅可用作伍尔芙研究的资料，其他许多不同学科——妇女研究、性别研究、酷儿研究、文学理论、女权主义研究——也可用其作为研究对象。正如伍尔芙研究专家、女性文学理论家苏珊·古芭尔指出的，它"在女权主义运动史上已经是一部经典之作——不说其为奠基之作的话"。[9]也正如亚历克斯·兹沃德林所言，该文本获得成功的首要一点是，伍尔芙具有小说家的"观察力和预测力，因此，才能对先前的女权主义作家遗留下的、未经展开的地方进行深究"。[10]1928年妇女赢得选举权，这一事件使她认识到，"为践行某一政治行为，必须具备简单化的激进思维，之后，认识问题的思维重新再复杂化"。[11]也就是说，《一间自己的房间》综合运用小说、文学批评、历史分析的手法，暴露了一些其他方面尚有待揭示的热点和问题。

局限性

虽然伍尔芙在《一间自己的房间》中提出的许多问题仍让今天的女权主义者和文学批评家着迷，但文本依然具有时代烙印。尽管伍尔芙敏锐地觉察到，在历史上，社会用各种方式制造了女性沉默的事实，并对此持批评态度，但是《一间自己的房间》对历史上其他被迫沉默与被压迫的群体却不感兴趣。在20世纪初期的英国，写作是上层白人阶层生活的一部分，伍尔芙仅解决白人女性的困境，而一旦涉及其他肤色和阶级的女性时，伍尔芙则熟视无睹。

　　伍尔芙的论述深入地关注物质生活和经济安全的重要性，但她的潜在读者对象是一群性别上虽然受到了歧视，但大多出身于上流阶层且拥有特权的女性。伍尔芙像书中的叙述人一样，属于这样一个阶层：大概可以继承每年 500 镑遗产。出身于工人阶层的英国妇女就没有这么好的运气，她们承受着既是女性又是英国"下层阶级"的双重重压。伍尔芙对和她出身相同的女性说，即便她们无法掌控自己的声音和命运，也不必害怕贫困。

　　伍尔芙倾听沉默者声音的方式已证明，首先她忽视了种族的语境，其次是缺少对肤色的论述。美国黑人作者和活动家爱丽丝·沃克 *，在其文章《寻找母亲们的花园》中，批评伍尔芙对非白人女性缺乏关注。从她的文章题目就可看出，爱丽丝·沃克如伍尔芙一样看重女性传统——她"母亲的"——但是她的传统严格地说是非洲裔美国女性传统。她的"母亲们"是指那些女性奴隶们，如早期非洲裔美国诗人菲莉丝·惠特利 *（1753—1784）。与 18 世纪白人相比，惠特利不奢望年收入接近 500 镑，不奢望有一间自己的房间，她所遭受的压迫甚至比 18 世纪的白人女性还要残酷：作为一名女奴，她"甚至连自己都无法拥有自己"。[12] 沃克在论文中发现了惠特利周围沉默的黑人妇女，建构了她自己的另一种历史的声音，这种历史的声音长期遭到殖民社会的压制。

1　见阿诺德·贝内特："高贵的女王"（《一间自己的房间》书评），《伦敦晚报》，1929 年 11 月 28 日，载《弗吉尼亚·伍尔芙：批评的遗产》，罗宾·马吉达尔和

艾伦·麦克劳林编，伦敦：劳特利奇出版社，1975年，第259页。

2　弗吉尼亚·伍尔芙：《一间自己的房间》和《三枚旧金币》，安娜·斯奈思编，牛津：牛津大学出版社，2015年，第81页。

3　贝内特："高贵的女王"，第259页。

4　伍尔芙：《一间自己的房间》，第3页。

5　伍尔芙：《一间自己的房间》，第3页。

6　赫尔迈厄尼·李：《弗吉尼亚·伍尔芙》，伦敦：温特吉出版社，1997年，第558页。

7　朱莉娅·布里格斯：《弗吉尼亚·伍尔芙：内在生活》，奥兰多：哈考特出版社，2005年，第235页。

8　见"文本注释"，载《一间自己的房间》，伍尔芙，第xxxvii页。

9　苏珊·古芭尔："前言"，载《一间自己的房间》，弗吉尼亚·伍尔芙著，苏珊·古芭尔编，奥兰多：哈考特出版社，2005年，第xxxvi页。

10　亚历克斯·兹沃德林：《弗吉尼亚·伍尔芙与真实的世界》，柏克利：加州大学出版社，1986年，第216页。

11　兹沃德林：《弗吉尼亚·伍尔芙与真实的世界》，第217页。

12　爱丽丝·沃克：《寻找母亲的花园：女性主义散文集》，伦敦：菲尼克斯出版社，2005年，第235页。

8 著作地位

要点

- 弗吉尼亚·伍尔芙是一位高产的作家，既写小说也写评论，以其擅长细致描写人生体验而著名。

- 虽然《一间自己的房间》在伍尔芙成就卓著的写作生涯中只是一个短篇，但在当时非常成功，且至今也是伍尔芙最著名的评论著作。

- 总体而言，伍尔芙的声誉主要还是在小说方面，她的小说位居 20 世纪小说史前列。如今，她最著名的代表作是《灯塔》（1925）和《达洛维夫人》（1927）。

定位

《一间自己的房间》仅是弗吉尼亚·伍尔芙众多著作中的一本。伍尔芙是一位高产的作家，擅长写各种体裁：除了 1915 至 1937 年间出版的 9 部小说，以及她自杀后于 1941 年出版的《幕间》，她还写过短篇小说、学术随笔和书评。仅学术随笔辑成的集子就有 6 部之多。去世后她的声名持续远扬，被公认为 20 世纪最伟大的作家之一，在小说史、现代主义发展史和女性写作史上，也是一位关键性人物。

在写作《一间自己的房间》之前，伍尔芙已经是一位名声在外的小说家，被公认为擅长细致描写人生体验和个人对外部世界的心理感受。《远航》（1915）讲述了一位年轻妇女到南美去旅行，在船上与其他游客交流过程中，思想受到启发并逐渐觉悟的故事。《夜与日》（1919）讲述了女性如何争取到投票的权益，作者把现代女性所面临的社会挑战和过去"伟大的男性形象"如何被偶像化进行关联。

而伍尔芙20世纪20年代出版的小说如《雅各的房间》(1922)、《达洛维夫人》(1925)、《到灯塔去》(1927)最受读者和研究者青睐。这3部小说探讨了个体经验与群体经验之间的关联和相互影响,而这一关系是通过人物在某个国家,某座城市和某个家庭中的经历形塑的。1928年,伍尔芙出版了《奥兰多:一部传记》,塑造了一个无与伦比的多重性别的主人公,并讲述了他长达几百年的生活经历。伍尔芙借此书讽刺了传统自传体小说。

在《一间自己的房间》里,伍尔芙说话语气不容置疑,俨然是一位权威小说家。该文本探讨了女权主义主题,并在其随后的学术随笔如《女性的职业》(1931)和《三枚旧金币》(1938)中继续探讨这一主题。《一间自己的房间》所探讨的问题,既是她绝大多数小说的核心主题,也是她后期评论的重点,可见该文本在她著作中的重要性。

> "我根本没有把你的成就只限定在小说上。如果你想让我开心——像我这样的人有上千个——你可写写旅游和冒险方面的书,写写研究类和论著类的书,写写历史和自传,写写批评、哲学和科学类的书。通过写作,你会窥探到小说的艺术。因为书籍也会相互影响。"
>
> ——弗吉尼亚·伍尔芙:《一间自己的房间》

整合

《一间自己的房间》以小说的笔法,通过以叙述人讲述生动的生活经历的方式提出问题。很显然,这一手法与她撰写其他作品的手法一致。她的小说，尤其是 1920 年代以后创作的小说，都采用了意识流 * 的现代主义手法。与之前传统的写作手法，如许多维多利亚时期小说使用的全知叙述人手法比较而言，这样的叙述声音更加流畅，允许读者从某个人物或者某几个人物的视角，"看见"小说中发生的各种事件。在伍尔芙的小说中，对人物内心生活（她们的各种想法，各种情绪以及各种记忆）的细节描写非常生动，其程度不亚于对人物的外部生活经历的描写，或者对人物关系的描写。

为了与传统叙述人的叙述方式一较高低——伍尔芙指出，传统叙述人会给出"纯粹的真理"——伍尔芙创造了一个虚构的叙述人，这一手法使得《一间自己的房间》与伍尔芙其他的小说构成一个整体。读者解读该文本的方式，要与解读《达洛维夫人》和《到灯塔去》一样："谎言从我唇间流出"，伍尔芙对他们说，"但谎言中有可能掺杂着真实，你的任务就是从中找出真实的部分"。[1] 换言之，就是鼓励读者积极地参与到文本的建构中，而不只是做一场讲座中"被动"的听众。

《一间自己的房间》的主题也与伍尔芙的其他作品一致，它们共同构成一个整体。她在篇幅更长的学术论文《三枚旧金币》（1938）中，重返女权主义这个话题，整部作品充满批评的话语。但早在 1929 年前后，她就在小说中广泛提及了女性选举权益和妇女运动的话题。在《夜与日》（1919）中，玛丽·达契特是一位努力争取选举权的活动家。她负责文书方面的工作，撰写宣传手册，负责妇女权利组织讨论小组的工作事宜。在《岁月》（1937）中，罗斯·帕吉特是位"妇女参政者"*，为赢得投票权被迫卷入了一场腥风血雨的激进主义运动中。[2]

意义

如今，《一间自己的房间》至少在两个不同的领域具有重要价值。在伍尔芙研究中，如果说伍尔芙的思想与女权主义的核心话题有着关联的话，那么该文本的细节就是最明显例证。尽管文本采用小说式叙述手法，但是与伍尔芙其他小说中涉及的妇女运动话题相比，该文本的叙述至今被认为是最为直接的。伍尔芙是英国文学史上最重要的作家，这一声誉与《一间自己的房间》关系不密切，应归功于她创作的几部里程碑式的小说。不过，如果想透彻理解伍尔芙的女权主义观点，《一间自己的房间》是重要的文本，读者常常把伍尔芙放置在 20 世纪初期女性作者的语境中进行解读。在伍尔芙所有作品中，该文本仅是一部小作品。

但这一点并不妨碍《一间自己的房间》在文学史和女权主义运动史中的重要性：把对妇女问题关注的重心从法律权益转移到了更加广泛的社会和心理问题上——尤其是父权制对个体妇女的精神摧残——文本预测了女权主义思想在 20 世纪后半期的主要发展方向。在伍尔芙时代（后来她的时代被命名为第一波女权主义时代）*，妇女运动关注的是在法律上和政治上赢得胜利，二战 * 后第二波女权主义 * 把关注的重心转移到了各种心理和文化问题上，而伍尔芙在文本中都论及了这些。有批评家提出，《一间自己的房间》完全不论及作者不赞成的观点。但即便如此，因为这个文本，凡是在与女权主义、妇女和文学相关的话题中，伍尔芙必然"占据着舞台的中心位置"，这是劳拉·马库斯的一大发现。[3]

1 弗吉尼亚·伍尔芙：《一间自己的房间》和《三枚旧金币》，安娜·斯奈思编，牛津：牛津大学出版社，2015 年，第 4 页。

2 继续延伸阅读，探究伍尔芙与妇女运动的关系，见索文·帕克：《选举权与弗吉尼亚·伍尔芙：单声背后的众生》，《英语研究评论》第 56 卷，2005 年第 223 期，第 119—134 页。

3 劳拉·马库斯：《弗吉尼亚·伍尔芙》第 2 版，塔维斯托克：诺思科特出版社，2004 年，第 41 页。

第三部分：学术影响

9 最初反响

要点 🗝—

- 《一间自己的房间》甫一出版，对其批评便集中在作品的主要观点上，并批评弗吉尼亚·伍尔芙迂回的写作方式偏离了核心论点。

- 伍尔芙没有回应批评，不过随后撰写的《三枚旧金币》更加直接地表达了她的女权主义观点，被看作是《一间自己的房间》的姐妹篇。

- 自作品出版以来，伍尔芙的文学声誉促使着读者按照自己的理解解读该作品。如今，该作品已被公认为女性主义文学史上重要的一环。

批评

　　1929 年弗吉尼亚·伍尔芙的《一间自己的房间》出版，当时没有收到太多的批评反馈。出版之前，伍尔芙有些担忧这篇集虚构和批评于一体的写作手法，以及以相当间接的方式接近主要问题的文章，不会"被认真对待"。[1] 她期待着男性评论家们屈尊作出评论，原本以为他们会称赞她的写作风格和"非常具有女性特征的逻辑"，然后推荐这本书"女孩们该人手一册"。[2]

　　现实和伍尔芙的预测接近。一位匿名评论家在著名的文学报刊《时代文学副刊》上发表书评，称其为"悠闲小品"，意指她游离于中心命题之外，且"兴致极好"。[3] 著名的文学批评家兼小说家阿诺德·贝内特也同样屈尊称赞了伍尔芙的写作风格——"她能写"——他说，文中迂回的风格是个巧合。伍尔芙不能直击核心，是由于她"是过于丰富想象力的受害者"。[4]然而，文章的"主题"——也就是女人需要年收入 500 英镑，并拥有一间自己的、能上锁的房间，才能够写小说——有争议性。[5]为了证明这一点，他以自己和俄国小说家费奥多尔·陀思妥耶夫斯基为例，指出他们既没有钱也没有一间自己的房间，而忽略了文中其他有关女性更宽泛的问题。

除此之外，《一间自己的房间》受到了批评家的称赞。一位当代批评家希望将来的女权主义者去阅读这个作品，他写道："伍尔芙看问题的视角不同于传统女权主义者。从那些老生常谈且激烈的冲突中，伍尔芙夫人提出了一个全新的问题，并提供解决的办法，发表自己的看法。"[6]她的解决办法和对此问题的看法将继续为之后的女权主义者解读该作品提供思路。

"我接收到的将只有那些委婉、幽默式的善良言语，没有任何的批评……出版社将非常善意友好，尽说些令人着迷、愉快的话；当然，我也可能因为是女权主义者将面临攻击，或被认为是女同性恋……我会收到好多好多年轻妇女写给我的信。我担心没有人把这场演讲当回事。伍尔芙女士的创作已经很成功，她说什么都会有人阅读的。"

——弗吉尼亚·伍尔芙:《作家日记》

回应

尽管正如伍尔芙所预计的那样，那些自视甚高的男性评论家，如阿诺德·贝内特对其作品作出了傲慢的评价，但《一间自己的房间》销量却极好。事实上，这本书的销量至今位居她所有书的首位。书的畅销是她能经济独立的主要支撑，同时也给她带来了文学上的声誉。[7] 书出版之后，伍尔芙从未对评论和批评作出过任何回应，她把发声权留给了书本身。

然而，在某种程度上，伍尔芙早在书出版之前就已经对可能会出现的负面批评表过态。从书的手稿可看出，伍尔芙对于可能引起的批评、读者可能的反应以及这本书可能给她造成的影响十分敏感。她以演讲稿为底稿，删去了一些激进的言论和对某些作者的否定评价，并且设置了一个虚构人物（也就是虚构的她）来替她发声。作家兼文学研究专家苏珊·古芭尔指出，伍尔芙"担心自己言辞太过犀利"，也担心因"女权主义者或是女同性恋的身份而遭到拒绝"，因此，采取各种办法确保不被拒绝。[8] 这些修改给作品披上了一层令人琢磨不透且也有趣的面纱，同时也增添了文本的丰富性。

之后的各种评论更倾向于明确称赞《一间自己的房间》中女权主义和女同性恋内涵。不确定性确保了各种可能且有效的阐释。如苏珊·古芭尔所言，该作品现在"在女权主义运动史上已经是一部经典之作——不称其为奠基之作的话"。因为从心理、社会、经济、意识形态等各个方面，它深刻地预测到了第二波女权主义运动浪潮所关注的核心问题。[9]

冲突与共识

在伍尔芙研究界、女性主义文学理论界以及女权主义研究等领域，《一间自己的房间》依然是广泛引起争论的文本。虽然人们普遍认为该文本"毋庸置疑是伍尔芙对文学批评和理论领域的重大贡献"，是女权主义思想史上重要的文本，但伍尔芙在这个文本里究竟想表达什么，她的思考模式是否能够成为当代的典范一直没有定论。[10] 如劳拉·马库斯所说，"伍尔芙被各个领域的评论家引用，被他们阐释，在不同的领域扮演着不同的角色，这本身就奠定了她如今的地位"。[11]

1938 年，伍尔芙写了《三枚旧金币》，表达她对女权主义问题的看法，此文一开始就被认为是《一间自己的房间》的姐妹篇。《一间自己的房间》出版 10 年后，《三枚旧金币》再一次探讨了女性表面上获得的法律权益与实际上社会赋予她们的物质条件之间的裂缝。然而在这个作品里，伍尔芙不再关注文本的创造性表达和艺术效果，转而关心政治媒介（自由）。《一间自己的房间》批判了父权制给女性带来的精神压迫。《三枚旧金币》回到这个主题，却更直接地强调了社会必须要赋予女性拥有能公开露面，能工作，拥有与男人一样平等的权利。当时，二战临近，《三枚旧金币》还直接把父权制度与消耗性冲突关联起来——传达的政治信息比《一间自己的房间》所表达的观点要直接得多。

虽然《三枚旧金币》的语气更加精确，但《一间自己的房间》仍是了解伍尔芙女权主义观点的主要文本，也是她贡献于女权主义运动的主要文本。正因如此，对该文本的争论依然没有停止，新一代女性主义思想家对该文本的诠释也没有停止。

---

1 弗吉尼亚·伍尔芙：《作家日记》，伦纳德·伍尔夫编，伦敦：哈考特出版社，1954 年，第 148 页。

2 伍尔芙：《作家日记》，第 148 页。

3 见罗宾·马吉达尔和艾伦·麦克劳林编：《弗吉尼亚·伍尔芙：批评的遗产》，伦敦：劳特利奇和基根·保罗，1975 年，第 255、256 页。

4 马吉达尔和麦克劳林编：《弗吉尼亚·伍尔芙：批评的遗产》，第 258、259 页。

5 马吉达尔和麦克劳林编：《弗吉尼亚·伍尔芙：批评的遗产》，第 259 页。

6 马吉达尔和麦克劳林编：《弗吉尼亚·伍尔芙：批评的遗产》，第 260 页。

7 赫尔迈厄尼·李：《弗吉尼亚·伍尔芙》，伦敦：温特吉出版社，1997 年，第 557 页。

8 见苏珊·古芭尔："前言"，载《一间自己的房间》，伍尔芙著，苏珊·古芭尔编，奥兰多：哈考特出版社，2005 年，第 xxxvii 页。或见弗吉尼亚·伍尔芙：《妇女与小说：〈一间自己的房间〉手稿本》，S.P. 罗森鲍姆编，牛津：布莱克威尔，1992 年。

9 古芭尔："前言"，第 xxxvi 页。

10 简·古德曼：《剑桥弗吉尼亚·伍尔芙导读》，剑桥：剑桥大学出版社，2006 年，第 97 页。

11 劳拉·马库斯：《弗吉尼亚·伍尔芙》第 2 版，塔维斯托克：诺思科特出版社，2004 年，第 41 页。

10 后续争议

要点 🔑

- 战后时期，第二波女权主义运动兴起。该运动致力于设法在更广的范围里确保女性的公民和文化地位，与此同时，弗吉尼亚·伍尔芙的主要观点，即妇女的物质生活条件大大地影响了女性创造艺术能力的发挥，被广泛接受。

- 虽然第二波女权主义运动的发起是多方面的影响所致，但在许多思想和论争方面，《一间自己的房间》都是其重要先驱。

- 近几年，伍尔芙文中提出的观点被应用到新的语境中，证明其观点适用于很多场域，这是伍尔芙没有预料到的。

应用与问题

弗吉尼亚·伍尔芙的《一间自己的房间》在女性主义文学理论中既存在争论又具有影响力。二战以后，第二波女权主义的热潮悄悄袭来。伍尔芙时代的第一波女权主义，争取的是法律、接受大学教育和工作的权益。第二波女权主义浪潮与此形成对照，关注的面更加广，而这些与伍尔芙在《一间自己的房间》中提出的观点和问题十分相似。

第二波女权主义关注的重心是父权制影响的广泛性和负面性。伍尔芙在《一间自己的房间》里生动地描述了英国男性从上至下享受着的特权，描述了他们对女性的隔绝，这些都引起了她们的共鸣。同时，尤其是法国的女性主义运动渐渐地转移目标，关注把社会当作由符号和语言所构成的"文本"*（如可读的）并加以讨论，这一点与伍尔芙考察女权主义的传统和其文字表述不谋而合。尤其是文中所言"如果女性像男性一样写作，那是极可悲的"（尽管与后面的观点矛盾），[1] 预示了 20 世纪 70 和 80 年代女性主义理论的一个重要主题——海伦·西克苏 * 所提出的"女性本色"或称作"女性写作"。[2]

同时，随着女性主义思想发生变化，《一间自己的房间》也遭受到批评，其中美国女性主义文学批评家伊莱恩·肖瓦尔特 * 的批评较有影响力。可以说肖瓦尔特的《她们自己的文学》（1977）就是一部揭伍尔芙短的长篇著作。直到 20 世纪 80 年代，几位颇有影响的评论家如挪威的陶丽·莫依 * 才恢复了伍尔芙的声誉。

> "许多男性批评家都说伍尔芙是个孩子气重、放荡不羁的文化人 *，在布卢姆斯伯里团体 * 里她是一位微不足道的唯美主义者。这一点也不奇怪，但这位伟大的女性主义作家不被英美女性主义后辈所接受，这一现象需要深入地作出解释。"
>
> ——陶丽·莫依：《性别 / 文本政治》

思想流派

女性主义文学学者简·古德曼指出，20 世纪 70 年代，每当女性主义者们作理论论争时，常常以《一间自己的房间》作为参考。尤其是文本从文化唯物主义角度讨论女性遭受的压迫——从日常生活的影响和经济状况的角度考察——被马克思主义女权主义者们所接受，认为这一观点论证了女性受资本主义社会和经济系统支配下的工作方式的压迫，有力地证明了马克思主义理论与女性处境的关系。[3]伍尔芙研究者简·马库斯在其著作《艺术与愤怒：像妇女一样阅读》（1988）和《弗吉尼亚·伍尔芙与男权制语言》中都证实了这些诠释。

然而，肖瓦尔特在《她们自己的文学》中指出，女性主义者同样可以拿"文化唯物主义"观点来反对伍尔芙，甚至以此反驳那些认为伍尔芙不是女权主义者的女性主义者们。对肖瓦尔特而言，是否存在具体的"女性"写作方式很值得研究。伍尔芙受到争议的地方在于，她"一头栽进雌雄同体"——因为她不寻求做女人，所以也不是个真正的女权主义者。[4]肖瓦尔特认为，《一间自己的房间》与其说是为女性真正自由的发声铺平道路，倒不如说是引领女性进入一个"无依无性的空间"——一个脱离社会，性别被剥夺的地方。[5]

虽然肖瓦尔特的批评得到了想定义女性特性的女权主义者们的支持，但也很快就遭到质疑。著名的理论家陶丽·莫依推崇弹性化的"女性"和女性声音概念，在出版于1985年的著作《文本/性别政治》中，她对上述观点进行了反驳。莫依巧妙地指出，如果女权主义理论家无法正确使用"（20世纪）最伟大的英国女作家的作品"，那么"这样的过错应归咎于她们自己的批评视角和理论依据"。[6]

当代研究

《一间自己的房间》是研究伍尔芙的关键文本，也是女权主义史和文论史上的重要文本。但这并不等于说，有关文本意义能达成简单的共识。伍尔芙从虚构的叙述者角度进行叙述，且只谈论女性需要资产和隐私的问题，引发了许多不一样的阐释——甚至是争论。伍尔芙研究专家、女性文学理论家苏珊·古芭尔*指出，批评家有时给它贴上女权主义的标签，有时给它贴上反女权主义*的标签——"漫画式笔法描绘男人使人生气""胆怯的愤怒""类马克思主义者"和"精英主义"。[7]这些争论表明了《一间自己的房间》的价值，争论源于文本的复杂性和文笔的深奥，也源于对作者和文本内容的不同态度。

陶丽·莫依恢复了伍尔芙在女性文学理论中的重要性，给其他女权主义理论家提供了一种解读的视角，自此确保了《一间自己的房间》在文学和女权主义研究中的地位。尤其是两本与此相关的专著的出版标志着该领域取得的成就：文学研究教授马基科·曼努·平克尼的《弗吉尼亚·伍尔芙与主体问题》（1987）和英语文学教授拉切尔·鲍尔比*的《弗吉尼亚·伍尔芙与女权主义者的使命》（1988年，1997年与另外5篇学术论文结集重版）。[8]前者把伍尔芙与法国女权主义结合在一起进行研究；后者对伍尔芙的女权主义作心理分析*式阅读，对其作品的开放性和意义的流动性作个案研究。

自20世纪90年代起，由于文学研究中开始出现同性恋女性主义和酷儿*理论热，人们依然阅读并讨论《一间自己的房间》，甚至阅读的人比过去还多。最近评论家们更多地是从性取向的不稳定性方面去解读该文和伍尔芙的作品，如爱琳·巴雷特和帕特丽夏·克莱默的论文集《弗吉尼亚·伍尔芙：同性恋阅读》仍然有影响力。

1　弗吉尼亚·伍尔芙：《一间自己的房间》和《三枚旧金币》，安娜·斯奈思编，牛津：牛津大学出版社，2015年，第66页。

2 参见海伦·西克苏：《美杜莎的笑》，基思和宝拉·科恩译，《标识》第 1 卷，
　1976 年第 4 期，第 875—893 页。

3 简·戈德曼：《剑桥弗吉尼亚·伍尔芙导读》，剑桥：剑桥大学出版社，2006 年，
　第 130 页。也可见弗吉尼亚·伍尔芙：《女性与写作》，米歇尔·巴雷特编，伦
　敦：妇女出版社，1979 年。

4 伊莱恩·肖瓦尔特：《她们自己的文学：从夏洛特·勃朗特到多丽丝·莱辛》，
　普林斯顿：普林斯顿大学出版社，1999 年，第 263 页。

5 肖瓦尔特：《她们自己的文学》，第 285 页。

6 陶丽·莫依：《文本 / 性别政治：女性主义文学理论》第 2 版，伦敦：劳特利奇
　出版社，2002 年，第 9 页。

7 伍尔芙：《一间自己的房间》，第 viii 页。

8 马基科·曼努-平克尼：《弗吉尼亚·伍尔芙与主体问题》，爱丁堡：爱丁堡大学
　出版社，2010 年；拉切尔·鲍尔比：《女权主义者的使命与弗吉尼亚·伍尔芙的
　研究论文》，牛津：布莱克威尔出版社，1997 年。

11 当代印迹

要点 🔑

- 在当今的伍尔芙研究领域和女性主义动史中,《一间自己的房间》依然是重要的文本。

- 文本论述了日常社交中的排外主义和物质条件的匮乏对女性的深刻影响,具有说服力,激发了读者从女性主义角度思考她们自己的生活经历。

- 虽然如今社会和物质条件发生了天翻地覆的变化,但它有关社会和物质条件影响了女性的生活与创造力的观点至今仍有意义。

地位

毫无疑问,弗吉尼亚·伍尔芙的《一间自己的房间》至今还是文学系学生的必读文本。用文学理论家陶丽·莫依的话说,伍尔芙是"(20)世纪英国最伟大的女作家",这一评价对该文本在文学经典中占据一席之地功不可没。该文本在伍尔芙文学事业的发展过程和在英国现代主义的发展史上也很重要。甚至有些理论家们,如极具影响力的女性主义学者伊莱恩·肖瓦尔特,虽不赞成伍尔芙的研究方法和观点,但也认为该文本在女性文学史上是一座里程碑。

在批评界,《一间自己的房间》一直处在争论中,其主要原因是文本的丰富性和复杂性。文本的论点简单且虚构性强,但其开放式结尾使得文本的价值不再仅仅是论点,还一直吸引着学界进行研究,甚至进行修改、完善。文本的形式和涉及的相关主题也一直具有影响力。当代许多女性主义批评著作要么直接引用伍尔芙的文本,要么模仿伍尔芙的写作风格，要么从伍尔芙的文本中获取思想的灵感，其中美国女性主义文学批评家苏珊·古芭尔的《我们自己的房间》（2006）最具有代表性。[1] 在文学和女性主义研究领域，伍尔芙至今还是一位重要人物，并且，尽管《一间自己的房间》在她丰厚的著作里仅是一本薄薄的小册子，但仍然是一本最重要的著作。

在学术圈外，《一间自己的房间》还在发挥着影响力。其中，2003 年，诺贝尔奖获得者南非作家 J.M. 库切 * 出版小说《伊丽莎白·卡斯特洛》。该小说主要就是受伍尔芙《一间自己的房间》全新的混合式表现形式的启发，叙述主人翁跟着一位女小说家到不同的地方发表一系列虚构演讲的故事。

> "尽管很明显地可以看出，伍尔芙的《一间自己的房间》和《三枚旧金币》（程度上不如前者）激发了我的灵感，当然，批评叙事的视角早就发生了转变。"
>
> ——苏珊·古芭尔:《我们自己的房间》

互动

苏珊·古芭尔《我们自己的房间》受到了众多女性主义批评家的影响，其中影响较大的是伍尔芙和她的《一间自己的房间》。古芭尔坦陈伍尔芙是其作品的中心。在《我们自己的房间》里，她对接受伍尔芙在作品中使用的混合着批评和小说化的叙述手法作了交代。小说描述了主人翁跟着一位美国大学的英语教授生活一年的经历，这一手法直接受到了前者的启发，而古芭尔给她的叙述人玛丽·贝顿洗礼的情节，与伍尔芙的叙述如出一辙。

《我们自己的房间》既思考了女性在当代的日常经验，也思考了一些从伍尔芙时代延续至今的一系列核心问题："区分了性与性别，区分了生物学意义上的生殖器与社会的角色，区分了来自于男性性别的男性化特征与来自于女性性别的女性化特征。"[2] 古芭尔让她的叙述人清晰地以伍尔芙的方式言说，表明自伍尔芙时代以来女性主义发生了多大的变化，以及伍尔芙的批评方法究竟有多大的影响。

库切受伍尔芙的影响稍弱一点。在《伊丽莎白·科斯特洛》中，库切塑造了一位澳大利亚小说家，作者跟着她到处发表演讲。讲座内容涉及很多方面，包括动物的权利。刚一读到小说开始部分，读者就会发现，在科斯特洛的生活中伍尔芙对她的影响较大，她像伍尔芙一样被迫去思考一些"大问题"，包括"妇女问题"。[3] 伍尔芙对库切的影响主要体现在小说的创作上：小说不只是描写讲座，准确地说是由讲座组成。"伊丽莎白·科斯特洛"是库切用来在现实生活中发表演讲的人格面具，就像伍尔芙利用"玛丽·贝顿"一样。

持续争议

就像伊莱恩·肖瓦尔特在批评中指出的，与其发现的问题一样，《一间自己的房间》在写作的方法上颇受争议。陶丽·莫依注意到，肖瓦尔特和其他批评家都期待《一间自己的房间》能够提供一个"评判世界的恒定视角"。但是，除了叙述人，幽默和讽刺的文风，至今很难对文本作出定论。[4] 伍尔芙的写作手法依然存在争议，它不符合现有的政治和学术书写的成规。

库切《伊丽莎白·科斯特洛》也遭遇到了类似的批评。小说一开始就写他 1997—1998 年在普林斯顿大学的生活碎片，为坦纳的讲座（论述哲学与伦理学）写讲稿。与传统的讲座不同，库切只念了两则女小说家做讲座的小故事。初版的书名是《动物的生命》（1999），书中收录了 4 位哲学家对此小说的评论，文本的碎片化引起了争议。小说家和批评家大卫·洛奇*在评论《伊丽莎白·科斯特洛》时写道，读者感觉到"受阻"，"小说披了一层面纱，在其背后（库切）隐藏着他个人的身份"。[5]詹姆斯·伍德指出，哲学家彼得·辛格*指责库切在"逃避"。[6]像伍尔芙一样，库切的影响力体现在小说《伊丽莎白·科斯特洛》的主要技巧中，而批评家则希望库切不要借助于小说发声。

苏珊·古芭尔在《我们自己的房间》中采用"叙事批评"的方法时，就预料到会招致与伍尔芙同样的批评声。读者也许会说，"知识的每一点进步都离不开……脚注、审慎及明晰性……仔细推理和历史还原"。[7]她提出，尽管如此，"当多元的视野，相互矛盾的陈规，呼吁我们寻找更有效的方法来解决彼此交融的文化问题时"，伍尔芙的方法至今有效，也有必要。[8]她说，伍尔芙的研究方法至今仍有争议，但可能对我们理解今天所面临的重大问题来说很关键。

---

1 见苏珊·古芭尔：《我们自己的房间》，尚佩恩：伊利诺伊大学出版社，2006 年。

2 古芭尔：《我们自己的房间》，第 2 页。

3 J.M. 库切：《伊丽莎白·科斯特洛》，伦敦：温特吉出版社，2004 年，第 10 页。

4 陶丽·莫依：《文本／性别政治》第 2 版，伦敦：劳特利奇出版社，2002 年，第 9 页。

5 大卫·洛奇："打破平静：库切的《伊丽莎白·科斯特洛》"，《纽约书评》，2003 年 11 月 20 日，登录日期：2015 年 9 月 21 日，http://www.nybooks.com/articles/archives/2003/nov/20/disturbing-the-peace/。

6 詹姆斯·伍德："一只青蛙的生命：库切的 8 堂课"，《伦敦书评》第 25 卷，2003 年 10 月 23 日第 20 期，第 15 页。

7 古芭尔：《我们自己的房间》，第 217 页。

8 古芭尔：《我们自己的房间》，第 218 页。

12 未来展望

要点 ⚷⊢

- 鉴于伍尔芙《一间自己的房间》在文学史上的地位，以及其与当今一些重大问题仍然相关，可以说它在将来还会是一部重要的文本。
- 如同当今一样，将来，该文本将会持续吸引新的读者，并影响批评家、作家和女性主义思想家。
- 《一间自己的房间》在女性主义运动史和文学理论史上，依旧是一部重要的文本，也是一份难得的文献资料。

潜力

伍尔芙《一间自己的房间》在当今的文学研究和女性主义研究中依然占有一席之地似乎毋庸置疑。自1928年至今，尽管妇女的权利和社会自由改善了很多，伍尔芙的分析路径仍然有效且有影响力，即社会习俗和经济条件迫使妇女扮演着某类角色，并在物质、心理上压制着她们。文学批评家苏珊·古芭尔和小说家库切指出，文本至今存在影响，并为女性主义和其他一些非传统的伦理问题，提供了检验的方法。

确保《一间自己的房间》在女性主义经典文本中占有一席之地的一个原因，是伍尔芙作为小说家所具有的影响力。伍尔芙在英语世界是文学课程大纲中的固定人物。她被认定是小说革新第一人，是文学史中的重要作家。伍尔芙的作品最为直接地指出了20世纪初期女性写作的困境。该文本是理解伍尔芙成长的重要文献资料。

然而，不仅如此，还可以通过该文本解读和分析日常的物质生活对作家思维的影响——无论作家是不是女性，伍尔芙都想进行研究。

尽管文本无法脱离作者自身历史视角的限制，而且无法脱离某些惯习的认识，如年龄和地位（如把阶级和种族压迫视为常态），《一间自己的房间》在某些领域仍能激发研究者的灵感。女性主义已经在多方面有所发展，远远超出伍尔芙的想象，并成为了一个理论上更加复杂的领域：与性别研究、酷儿理论、后殖民理论＊相关联（对殖民主义从多方面进行理论探索）。但伍尔芙的文本仍是一座里程碑。

> "机会即将来临，死去的诗人、莎士比亚的妹妹过去一直躺在那儿，现在即将运动起自己的身体，步其兄长的后尘，从其先驱的生命中复生。她即将诞生。"
>
> ——弗吉尼亚·伍尔芙：《一间自己的房间》

未来方向

很难预测将来文学批评会从什么样的角度去解析《一间自己的房间》。显然，尽管考虑到批评伍尔芙"房间"有局限性的声音还在继续，努力让那些被环境和霸权（政治和文化上的控制）所遮蔽的作家重见天日的事情还在继续着，这个文本对未来的学术研究仍有意义。《一间自己的房间》的价值持续不退，正在于它坚持认为女性的生活不应该仅仅限定在家庭范围内，女性对于创造性或职业性，以及独立的生活方式的追求不但可能而且可行。

当今，在很多国家，女性和男性在就业机遇和经济条件上的差距确实缩小了很多。如今，英国女性可以追求学业，谋求个人的职业，从事那些具有创造性的工作，而不再会面临伍尔芙和她的首批读者所遇到的各种阻挠。但男性与女性之间的不平等，强势与弱势社会群体之间的差别依旧存在。在时代变化的激流中，传统上期待女性对家庭事务付出更多的想法依旧存在。从全球视野来看，与男性相比，女性在教育、职业和艺术上的机遇仍然受到很多狭隘的限制。《一间自己的房间》的现代性也鼓励着现在和未来对这些问题的探讨。

美国小说家爱丽丝·沃克运用伍尔芙的框架分析美国历史中黑人女性的境遇，发现伍尔芙的观点并不局限于她写作时所期待的读者。[1]《一间自己的房间》把物质条件和创造性劳动结合起来，为艺术生产所需的必要条件提供了一个非常有价值的范例。所有公民都能借助此文本赢得争取上述条件的权利——无论是女性还是其他在社会条件上受到压制的群体。

小结

今天，对小说的演变、女性写作或者女权主义感兴趣的人都应该阅读《一间自己的房间》，因为它不但具有历史价值且与当今的问题息息相关。它值得特别的关注，因为它融合了文学与批评的方法，它理性且有力地为女性声张权益，还因为它在伍尔芙著作中的地位，以及文本自身持续的张力。弗吉尼亚·伍尔芙的作品在当今文学经典中享有特殊的地位，被世界各地的学者研究着。她的现代主义小说以及她对文本类型、现代美学、社会问题的批评文章使她在英语文学中独树一帜。《一间自己的房间》的成功既代表了她在文学史上的地位，也说明了她在实现目标过程中遇到的挑战。

该文本有着特殊的历史背景，弗吉尼亚·伍尔芙的视角也有其自身的局限性。但这些局限性引发了更多的讨论，也突出了其基础价值。爱丽丝·沃克等批评家指出，其中心论点并不是为历史上所有女性代言，也不是为所有作家代言。但正因如此，他们不断拓展了伍尔芙的"房间"空间，使其适合于更多不同身份的人、发出更多不同的声音。这正是伍尔芙希望她的作品能起到的作用，这一点毋庸置疑。

在讨论《一间自己的房间》的经典地位和深刻内涵的同时，我们也不能忽略它的可读性。它不仅仅是一篇重要的文章，还是一部层层递进、内容丰富且充满说服力的文学作品，同时也是一段打开伍尔芙的文学世界和女权主义理论的绝美前奏。

---

1 参见爱丽丝·沃克：《寻找母亲的花园：女性主义散文集》，伦敦：菲尼克斯出版社，2005 年。

术语表

1. **反女权主义**：泛指意识形态上反对女权主义。

2. **雌雄同体**：该术语指生理和心理上同时拥有男性化和女性化两性特征。

3. **布卢姆斯伯里团体**：一个由一群有影响力的英国作家、艺术家、哲学家和学者组成的非正式团体，包括了弗吉尼亚·伍尔芙、约翰·梅纳德·凯恩斯、E. M. 福斯特等人，以英国伦敦布卢姆斯伯里广场和周边地区为活动中心。

4. **波西米亚风**：指称习性上与一般社会习俗迥异的一类人，尤其指拥护反传统或政治观点激进的作家、学者、艺术家和演员。

5. **文化唯物主义**：一场主张从物质生产条件的角度分析艺术作品的批评运动。虽然通常被认为是战后英国文学批评家雷蒙德·威廉斯的主要观点，但可以溯源于德国经济学政治哲学家卡尔·马克思（1818—1883）的著作当中。

6. **伊丽莎白时代**：1558 年至 1603 年，伊丽莎白一世女王统治英国的时期。

7. **女权主义**：为实现女性在性别阶层平等而发起的一系列运动和社会理论。

8. **第一波女权主义**：为争取与男性平等的法律权利，尤其是投票权，而于 19 世纪晚期至 20 世纪初期兴起的妇女运动，主要活跃于英国和北美地区。

9. **格顿学院**：剑桥大学的一个学院，建于 1869 年。曾为女子学院，直至 1976 年通过投票才决定开始招收男生。

10. **霍加斯出版社**：弗吉尼亚·伍尔芙和伦纳德·伍尔夫于 1917 年在里士满的霍加斯家中创办的出版社。因出版了弗吉尼亚自己的作品和 T. S. 艾略特的《荒原》第一版而闻名。

11. **文学正典**：指古往今来被学术界和学者认为是最具有影响力和价值的一系列文学作品。

12. **厌女症**：指对女性的憎恨和厌恶。

13. **现代主义**：认为艺术既应脱离传统模式的束缚又应承载传统艺术精髓的一场规模庞大的文艺运动。在文学领域，弗吉尼亚·伍尔芙、T. S. 艾略特、詹姆斯·乔伊斯等人在 20 世纪初的 30 多年中创作了一系列前所未有的文学作品而成为标杆。

14. **纽汉姆学院**：剑桥大学的一个学院，于 1871 年成立的女子学院，至今该学院依旧只招收女生。

15. **父权**：指男性掌握权力的核心，拥有特殊的权益，并具有权威性的社会体系。在女权主义理论看来，西方社会普遍都是父权社会。

16. **后殖民理论**：一种带有文化批判和哲学思考的话语场，主要探讨殖民主义和帝国主义在英国、法国、西班牙等西方国家的前殖民地区留下的文化和知识方面的影响。

17. **战后时期**：主要指欧洲和美洲在第二次世界大战结束之后的阶段。

18. **精神分析**：一系列关于治疗精神疾病的理论。最初由奥地利心理学家西格蒙德·弗洛伊德在 19 世纪末提出。

19. **酷儿理论**：涉及范围十分广泛的文化理论，主要通过文学研究、女性研究和文化研究来探讨和分析新性别认同问题。

20. **第二波女权主义**：战后女权主义社会运动。深受法国女权主义理论影响，主要关注女性性自由、生育权和工作权益等问题。

21. **意识流**：一种叙述技巧。模仿小说中人物的思维过程，通过人物的所思所感直接描绘人物对于外部事物的反应和感知。

22. **选举权**：指公开选举时拥有的投票权，特指第一波女权主义运动所关注的女性投票权。

23. **妇女参政者**：指 19 世纪和 20 世纪初在妇女运动中，为女性成员争取投票权（选举权）而开展运动的女性成员，特别指代较为激进的参政人员。

24. **文本的**：字面意义即像文本或者与文本有关的，作为隐喻的修辞常常用来描写哲学、社会学和文学理论中的社会，意思是社会结构能够像一本书或者一篇文本一样被"阅读"。

25. **剑桥大学**：于 1209 年建立，是英国第 2 所大学，由 31 个学院组成；通常被认为是世界上最负盛名的学校之一。

26. **妇女运动**：泛指妇女解放运动或女权运动。通常特指早期的女权主义和为妇女争取投票权的运动。

27. **第一次世界大战**：1914 至 1918 年间发生的全球冲突。冲突主要集中在欧洲由德国、奥地利、匈牙利组成的"轴心国"与由英国、法国与俄国组成的盟国之间。

28. **第二次世界大战**：1939 至 1945 年间发生的全球性战争，30 多个国家被卷入进来，冲突围绕着纳粹德国与其盟国所进行的扩张政策。

人名表

1. 简·奥斯汀（1775—1817），英国小说家，以对自己所生活的时代，对社会细微的观察和讽刺幽默的表述而闻名。她的小说创作中不乏被认为是英国经典文学之列的名篇，如《傲慢与偏见》（1813）和《爱玛》（1815）。

2. 阿芙拉·贝恩（约1640—1689），英国剧作家和诗人。她是英国戏剧界第一位重要的女作家，最早从事职业写作的女作家。至今仍然有名的作品是戏剧《漫游者》（分为两部分，分别创作于1677和1681年）和散文体小说《奥鲁诺克》（1688）。

3. 克莱夫·贝尔（1881—1964），英国艺术批评家和形式主义艺术理论的代言人。他是布卢姆斯伯里团体的成员，弗吉尼亚·伍尔芙的姐姐瓦内萨的丈夫。

4. 瓦内萨·贝尔（本姓斯蒂芬；1879—1961），英国画家、插画家、设计师；她是弗吉尼亚·伍尔芙的姐姐，也是布卢姆斯伯里团体的成员，克莱夫·贝尔的妻子。

5. 阿诺德·贝内特（1867—1931），英国小说家、记者和批评家。一位高产作家，1908年创作的小说《老妇人的故事》至今盛名不减。

6. 拉切尔·鲍尔比，普林斯顿大学英国文学教授。她最具影响力的学术著作是1988年出版的《弗吉尼亚·伍尔芙与女权主义者的使命》。

7. 勃朗特三姐妹，19世纪初期英国著名女作家。夏洛蒂（1816—1855）最为高产，其作品《简·爱》（1847）最受欢迎；艾米莉（1818—1848）仅一部小说《呼啸山庄》（1847）；安妮（1820—1849）创作了《艾格妮丝·格雷》（1847）和《荒野庄园的房客》（1848）两部小说。

8. 海伦·西克苏（1937年生），具有非凡影响力的法国女权主义作家和哲学家，被认为是后结构主义女权主义理论之母。1975年撰写的文章《美杜莎的笑》令她声名大噪，女性本色（"女性写作"）的概念也让她十分知名。

9. 爱德华·克拉克（1820—1877），医学博士，哈佛大学医学教授。他至今被人提及乃因其在著作《教育中的性：女孩的公平机会》（1873）中提出的女性教育的误导性观点。

10. J.M. 库切（1940 年生），诺贝尔奖获得者，南非小说家、散文家和翻译家。迄今他已创作了 12 部小说和 4 部小说体自传。他被认为是世界上仍然健在的著名小说家。

11. 费奥多尔·陀思妥耶夫斯基（1821—1881），俄国小说家，19 世纪最重要的作家。最著名的代表作有《罪与罚》（1866）和《卡拉马佐夫兄弟》（1880）。

12. 乔治·艾略特（1819—1880），小说家安妮·艾凡斯的笔名。被公认为小说史上最重要的一位作家。代表作有《佛罗斯河畔上的磨坊》（1860）和《米德尔马契》（1872）。

13. T.S. 艾略特（1888—1965），出生于美国的诗人和批评家，英国现代主义的开创人。最著名的作品有长诗《荒原》（1922）和《四个四重奏》（1945），以及著名的批评论文《传统和个人才能》（1919）。

14. E.M. 福斯特（1879—1970），英国小说家、散文家、文学批评家，布卢姆斯伯里团体成员之一。著有小说《印度之行》（1908）、《霍华兹庄园》（1910），以及以同性恋为主题的小说《莫瑞斯》（1971），实际上该书写于 1913 至 1914 年间，作者去世后才出版。

15. 罗杰·弗莱（1866—1934），英国画家和艺术批评家。他是布卢姆斯伯里团体成员之一，因诠释后印象派绘画而享有名誉。

16. 玛格丽特·福勒（1810—1850），美国记者和早期女权主义者，她的《19 世纪的妇女》（1843）被认为是美国最早的女权主义著作。

17. 夏洛特·帕金斯·吉尔曼（1860—1935），美国著名的女权主义者和作家。著作《女性与经济：社会演变中经济关系在男女关系中扮演的角色研究》（1898）是女权主义运动史中的经典文本。

18. 苏珊·古芭尔（1944 年生），美国作家、女权主义文学批评家，目前在印第安纳大学教授英语文学和女性研究。代表作是和桑德拉·M.吉尔伯特合写的《阁楼上的疯女人：女性作家和 19 世纪的文学想象》（1979）。

19. 西塞莉·汉密尔顿（1872—1952），英国女演员、作家和女权主义者，1908 年女性作家选举同盟会的合作创办人。

20. 詹姆斯·乔伊斯（1882—1941），爱尔兰小说家和现代主义运动的先驱者，最负盛名的作品有《尤利西斯》（1922）和《芬尼根的守灵夜》（1939）。

21. 约翰·梅纳德·凯恩斯（1883—1946），富有影响力的英国经济学家，他的宏观经济学理论颠覆了传统经济学说。

22. D.H. 劳伦斯（1885—1930），英国小说家、诗人和批评家。备受争议的小说《查泰莱夫人的情人》被认为是小说发展进程上的一个里程碑。

23. 大卫·洛奇（1935 年生），英国小说家和批评家。作为小说家，因多部小说以讽刺的笔调描写学术人的生活而著名；作为批评家，以文学批评，特别是论文集《小说的艺术》（1992）而著名。

24. 陶丽·莫依（1953 年生），出生于挪威的女权主义理论家和文学批评家。目前在美国杜克大学担任杰姆斯·B.杜克教授，教授英语文学、哲学和戏剧研究。代表作有《性别 / 文本政治：女性主义文学理论》（1985）、《什么是妇女及其他（论文集）》（1999）。

25. 艾兹拉·庞德（1885—1972），美国诗人。他的诗歌助推了现代主义运动的产生。最负盛名的作品是《诗章》（1917—1969），一部复杂且难懂的叙事诗。

26. 亚瑟·奎勒·库奇（1863—1944），英国作家和文学批评家。涉猎各种文类的创作，且都多有建树，以编纂《牛津英国诗选 1250—1900》（1900）而著名。

27. 埃莉诺·拉斯伯恩（1872—1946），英国女权主义者和议会独立成员，因长期投身于为英国女性争取权益的运动而知名。

28. 伊丽莎白·罗宾斯（1862—1952），美国女演员、剧作家，妇女参政权论者。1888 年移居英格兰后，投身于女权运动，创作了具有非凡影响力的剧本《为女性投票！》（1907）。

29. 薇塔·萨克维尔·韦斯特（1892—1962），诗人、小说家和记者，同时还是一名非常出色的园艺家。因和多位女性发生婚外情而出名。与弗吉尼亚·伍尔芙的一段过往成为伍尔芙的灵感源泉，后被写成小说《奥兰多：一部传记》。

30. 萨福（约公元前 630—570），古希腊著名女抒情诗人，生于莱斯波斯岛。虽然只有少数的作品被流传下来，但她为男人和女人创作的情诗家喻户晓。20 世纪中期开始，她的名字成为女同性恋的代名词。

31. 奥莉芙·施莱纳（1855—1920），南非作家，反战主义者，早期女权主义者。至今被人知晓的作品是小说《非洲农场的故事》（1883）和女权主义著作《妇女与劳工》（1911）。

32. 威廉·莎士比亚（1564—1616），英国诗人和剧作家。创作的 154 首十四行诗和 38 部剧本不但是英国文学研究的主要对象，也是不断被世界各地搬上舞台表演的"活文本"。被公认为英格兰民族诗人。

33. 伊莱恩·肖瓦尔特（1941 年生），美国女性文学批评家，提出了"女性中心批评"的概念。代表作有《女性诗学研究》（1979）和《发现自我：女性文学脉络实证》（2001）。

34. 彼得·辛格（1946 年生），澳大利亚道德哲学家，普林斯顿大学生物伦理学教授。他的代表作是 1975 年出版的《动物解放》，被公认为论述动物权利的经典著作。

35. 安德里安·斯蒂芬（1883—1948），弗吉尼亚·伍尔芙的弟弟，布卢姆斯伯里团体的成员。最早接受西格蒙德·弗洛伊德理论的一批人，也是英国最早的神经分析学家。

36. 莱斯利·斯蒂芬（1832—1904），英国学者、批评家、传记作者。弗吉尼亚·伍尔芙的父亲。《英国人物传记词典》首任主编，也因此闻名于世。

37. **托比·斯蒂芬**（1880—1906），弗吉尼亚·伍尔芙的哥哥，布卢姆斯伯里团体最初的召集人。

38. **里顿·斯特拉奇**（1880—1932），英国传记作家，布卢姆斯伯里团体成员，1918 年出版的《英国人之最：维多利亚》最广为人知。

39. **雷·斯特拉奇**（本名科斯特洛；1887—1940），英国女权主义政治家和作家。她是里顿·斯特拉奇的哥哥奥利弗的妻子，因参与选举运动以及 1928 年出版的作品《缘起：大英帝国妇女运动简史》而广为人知。

40. **爱丽丝·沃克**（1944 年生），美国作者、女权主义者、社会活动家。代表作有 1982 年出版的小说《紫色》和 1983 年出版的散文合集《寻找母亲的花园：女性主义散文集》。

41. **奥托·魏宁格**（1880—1903），奥地利哲学家。带有贬抑女性意味的著作《性与性格》（1903）在他自杀后受到了全世界的关注。

42. **菲莉丝·惠特利**（1753—1784），非裔美国诗人，第一位出版作品的非裔美国妇女。幼时被作为黑奴贩卖到美国，她的《不同主题、宗教与道德的诗》（1773）使她家喻户晓，也使她获得了终身自由。

43. **玛丽·沃斯通克拉夫特**（1759—1797），英国作家，哲学家。《女权辩》（1792）是其代表作，也是女权主义的奠基之作。

44. **伦纳德·伍尔夫**（1880—1969），1921 年与弗吉尼亚·伍尔芙结婚，直至她 1941 年去世。布卢姆斯伯里团体的成员，是一名出色的出版人和作家，与夫人一起创办了霍加斯出版社，并出版过多部政治理论方面的著作。

WAYS IN TO THE TEXT

- The British novelist and critic Virginia Woolf was born in 1882 and grew up in London. Her experiences as a female writer helped form her theories on literature and feminism*—an intellectual and political movement seeking equality between the sexes.

- *A Room of One's Own*, published in 1929, was innovative in its focus on the problems faced by women in day-to-day life and their effects on the mind, rather than on legal obstacles faced by women.

- *A Room of One's Own* is a vital document in the history of feminism. It still attracts a broad audience in and beyond academia, and remains influential in feminist literary criticism.

Who Was Virginia Woolf?

Virginia Woolf, the author of *A Room of One's Own*, was born in 1882 and grew up in the London district of Kensington in an upper-class intellectual household. She and her sister Vanessa did not attend school or university, like their brothers, but were educated at home instead; this was typical of attitudes at the time. In spite of this limitation, Woolf gained a better education than most women of the age. Her father—a journalist, historian, and biographer—had an extensive library and she had full access to it. As a result, Woolf gained a wide knowledge of literature, which was vital to her intellectual development.

Through her brothers, Thoby* and Adrian,* Woolf became friends in her youth with a group of intellectuals, artists, and writers later known as the Bloomsbury Group.* They met frequently at the house Woolf shared with her siblings in London's Bloomsbury

Square. Several of the Bloomsbury Group, including Woolf, were important innovators in the fields of art, literature, and economics. They were also fiercely independent thinkers who went against many of the standard codes of the age.

Woolf published her first novel in 1915, and went on to publish seven more before her death in 1941. Her final novel, finished shortly before her suicide, was published posthumously. Woolf's writing was successful in her own time, and she was regarded as one of the brightest lights in modern literature. Since her death, her reputation has continued to grow. She is considered one of the greatest novelists of the twentieth century.

What Does *A Room of One's Own* Say?

Despite her success and privileges, Woolf was still a woman born into a man's age. Her personal experiences of the limits placed on women by British society in the early twentieth century directly inform her 1929 essay *A Room of One's Own*. The essay asks two central questions: why have there been so few great women writers in history? And what does one need in order to write?

Woolf answers the second question first. Part of her answer gives the essay its title: to write, one must have a private room. The second part is that one must have money. Woolf settles on the figure of £500 a year—in 1929 a steady and comfortable income. These are necessary for writing, Woolf states, because writing depends on everyday life. In order to write, you must have privacy, and you must be free of worries about money. Only with privacy and security can a person create art.

This idea is a direct response to the way women lived in the early twentieth century. Though their legal rights were being increased, women still had fewer rights than men. There were restrictions on women's ability to own property and to be educated. There were also clear social expectations that placed limits on women. Marriage was regarded as a primary social goal and, once married, women were expected not to work. They were also expected to devote their lives to their husbands and children. As a result, married women generally had no income of their own, and no real privacy. Hence Woolf's demand for two simple things that many today would take for granted.

The first question—why have there been so few great women writers?—is more complicated. In the early twentieth century, women were routinely thought to be less intelligent than men, and the lack of famous women writers and artists in history was often presented as evidence of this. Woolf, however, assumes that women are just as intelligent as men and looks for other causes. If women have not written great books, she suggests, it is because something has prevented them.

What, though? In Woolf's analysis, society throughout history has created conditions in which no woman could write. Women have not had privacy, money, or education. Woolf suggests that even the most exceptionally talented woman could not write in such a society. It is not intellectual inferiority that has made it impossible for women to write literature—it is the conditions of everyday life.

Woolf also presents a third reason for the lack of great present-day female writers: the absence of famous female writers in history. She argues that female writers need a tradition of older female writers in order to produce great work. She encourages women in her own time to write, no matter what the subject, in order to create such a tradition. Only then, she argues, will future women be able to write great books.

Why Does *A Room of One's Own* Matter?

It is hard to overstate the importance of *A Room of One's Own* in the history of feminism. When Woolf wrote the essay in 1929, women in Britain were at a turning point. For the first time, they had full voting rights, and were breaking other legal barriers to equality. But much of the early feminist movement was focused on winning legal rights alone. Woolf's essay was a crucial reminder that inequality had deeper causes than unjust laws. In her view, women's lower status in society affected every area of their lives, and came from the smallest everyday conditions. *A Room* shifted the emphasis of feminism from legal battles to altering everyday life too.

Woolf clarified this focus by addressing a central question of literary criticism: what does it take to produce great art? In the early twentieth century, a majority of academics and critics believed that great art was a product of "genius." Such genius was assumed to be greater than any social barriers. It would express itself regardless of poverty, lack of education, or want of time and privacy. The absence of great women writers and artists in history was therefore seen as evidence that women could not be geniuses. This in turn justified social structures that treated them as less worthwhile than men. Woolf, however, turned her attention to the ways in which everyday life can stop even geniuses from producing great art. Although her focus was specifically on women, Woolf's views on how closely art is rooted in real life anticipate one of the major trends in twentieth-century criticism. *A Room of One's Own* helped fundamentally shift views of "artistic genius" in literary criticism and beyond.

Today, nearly 90 years after it was first published, *A Room of One's Own* remains a relevant and important text. Though life has improved for women in Britain and elsewhere over the last century, many of Woolf's arguments are still valid. Her portrayal of the effects of everyday life on the mind provides a useful framework for thinking about social groups suffering the effects of prejudice. For any reader interested in feminism or literary criticism it is a seminal text.

SECTION 1
INFLUENCES

MODULE 1
THE AUTHOR AND THE HISTORICAL CONTEXT

KEY POINTS

- *A Room of One's Own* is a crucial document in the history of the intellectual and social movement of feminism,* and one of the most influential pieces of twentieth-century feminist literary criticism.

- Virginia Woolf's upbringing gave her a privileged access to education but deprived her of the opportunities extended to her brothers.

- After the initial victories of first-wave feminism* (the feminist activism of the nineteenth and early twentieth century that largely focused on basic equalities under the law), Woolf saw that the battle for equality was as much about the basic conditions of life in British society as it was about legal rights.

Why Read This Text?

Virginia Woolf's *A Room of One's Own* (1929) is a seminal text in the history of feminist thought, by a writer regarded as the most important female novelist of the twentieth century. The essay helped expand the debate on women's equality beyond constitutional legal issues such as voting rights. It examined the deep psychological effects of the conditions of everyday life on women, and on female writers in particular.

The feminist debates of the early twentieth century had concentrated largely on the gaining of key legal rights for women—in particular women's suffrage* (the right to vote in national elections). But *A Room of One's Own* concentrated on the impact of daily life on women's psyches and talents. The essay tries to answer the question of why the literary canon* (the set of works generally agreed to be literary classics) contains so few works by women writers. Working from the cultural materialist* proposition that art is closely linked to "material" life—a person's economic circumstances, clothes, access to private space, interactions with other people—Woolf suggests that potential women writers throughout history have been prevented from writing by material conditions that persistently privilege men. How, Woolf asks, can history's women have been expected to produce literature when deprived of money, privacy, and education?

When *A Room of One's Own* was published it helped create a profound change in feminism. It is still an intellectually rich and thought-provoking work. Ahead of its time, its central themes became major questions for feminists throughout the second half of the twentieth century, and remain relevant today. Providing a vital insight into Virginia Woolf's own work as well as into early feminist thought, it remains a key text for students of literature and feminism.

> *"I am back from speaking at Girton,* in floods of rain. Starved but valiant young women—that's my impression. Intelligent, eager, poor; and destined to become schoolmistresses in shoals."*
>
> ——Virginia Woolf, *A Writer's Diary*

Author's Life

Virginia Woolf was born on January 25, 1882 in Kensington, London, the third child of Leslie Stephen* and Julia Stephen. Woolf's siblings were Vanessa* (born 1879), Thoby* (1880), and Adrian* (1883). Her brothers went to boarding school and later to the University of Cambridge;* the girls were home-schooled. In their father's library, however, they had access to a wide selection of books. Virginia gained a deep knowledge of English literature and the classics, which laid the ground for her development as a writer.

After their father's death in 1904, she and her siblings moved to Bloomsbury Square in London. There they became friends with the artists and intellectuals later known as the Bloomsbury Group.* Together with the Stephens, the group included the novelist E. M. Forster,* the economist John Maynard Keynes,* and the biographer Lytton Strachey,* among others. In 1912, Virginia married one of that circle, Leonard Woolf,* taking the name by which she became known.

Virginia Woolf's writing career began in 1900 with journalism, and she started work on her first novel in 1907. That book— *The Voyage Out* (published 1915)—was followed by eight more, including *Mrs Dalloway* (1925), *To the Lighthouse* (1927), and *The Waves* (1931). Of her nonfiction the best-known works remain *Modern Fiction* (1919) and *A Room of One's Own* (1929). Her books made Woolf a literary celebrity within her lifetime, and today she is accepted as one of the twentieth century's greatest writers.

In an age when literary fame and intellectual respect were rarely achievable for women, Woolf was acutely aware of the difficulties women faced, and the psychological consequences of being a talented woman in a generally misogynistic* (woman-hating) society. Subject to bouts of mental illness and suicide attempts throughout her life, Woolf committed suicide in 1941, shortly after completing her final novel, *Between The Acts*, which was published posthumously.

Author's Background

The 1920s were a pivotal time for Britain, for British women, and for the arts.[1] The United Kingdom was the major world power, maintaining an empire of approximately 450 million subjects— one-fifth of the world's population—and it reaped the economic benefits of its dominance.[2] Technological changes, such as radio, provoked a fascination with the possibilities of modern media, which began to have important effects on the arts and everyday life.[3] But at the same time, Britain was a wounded nation, suffering from the physical and psychological effects of World War I* (1914–18).

With over 700, 000 British servicemen dead—approximately 35 percent of males aged 19 to 22—the war caused huge social changes, particularly for women.[4] In 1918, women over 30 gained the right to vote. In 1928 this was extended to all women over 21 in a parliamentary act that was passed just two months before Woolf delivered the lectures upon which *A Room of One's Own* is based. Many of the female undergraduates whom Woolf addressed in 1928 were part of a new generation of young female students and women who were working outside the home in greater numbers than ever before.

There were still many obstacles to women's rights, however, and women remained vastly less valued than men by society, and vastly less materially well-off. At the time of Woolf's visit to Cambridge, for instance, female students were still not full members of the university. They would not be full members until 1948.[5]

---

1 For a concise, in-depth overview of Woolf's historical context see Michael H. Whitworth, *Virginia Woolf* (Oxford: Oxford University Press, 2005), ch. 2, passim.

2 Angus Maddison, *The World Economy: A Millennial Perspective* (Paris: Organisation for Economic Co-operation and Development, 2001), 98.

3 See Tapan K. Sarkar et al., *History of Wireless* (Hoboken, NJ: Wiley-Interscience, 2006).

4 See John Keegan, *The First World War* (New York: Vintage, 2000), 439.

5 For a full history see Rita McWilliams-Tullberg, *Women at Cambridge: A Men's University, Though of a Mixed Type* (London: Gollancz, 1975).

MODULE 2
ACADEMIC CONTEXT

KEY POINTS

- The position and lives of women in patriarchal* (male-dominated) society was, and remains, a central question in the intellectual and political movement of feminism.*

- While legal rights were the main focus of early feminism, the idea that repressive social conventions and lack of education contributed substantially to women's lower status had been present since the early feminist thinker Mary Wollstonecraft's* *Vindication of the Rights of Woman* (1792).

- Unlike many of her contemporaries, Virginia Woolf focused on the effects of everyday existence on women, particularly women writers, and suggested that these "material conditions" were of more significance than legal rights.

The Work in Its Context

Virginia Woolf's *A Room of One's Own* should be seen in three intellectual contexts: Woolf's own intellectual background, the history of feminism, and the history of literature.

Woolf benefited from personal ties to the literary and intellectual elite of the period. Her father, Leslie Stephen,* was a journalist, biographer, and historian of ideas, now best known for founding the *Dictionary of National Biography*. Thanks to his learning, Woolf grew up in a rich intellectual environment. Further links to the intellectual elite came through her brothers Adrian* and Thoby* Stephen who, at the University of Cambridge,* became friends with the gifted thinkers who later formed the core of the circle of intellectuals and artists known as the Bloomsbury Group.*

Feminism was also at a turning point intellectually. Increased rights for women were often met by a hardening of old social prejudices against them, and there were intense debates about the nature of women within feminist circles. As the English literature scholar Michael Whitworth points out, immediately after partial voting rights were achieved in 1918, divisions appeared between "old" and "new" feminism.[1] The former saw women as deserving equal rights because—as humans—they were essentially the same as men. The latter sought parity but emphasized gender difference. These debates lay behind *A Room*'s questioning of mental "androgyny"*—what it might mean to have a mind that is neither male nor female, or perhaps both.[2]

Lastly, during the first decades of the twentieth century the movement of modernism* had overturned and reinvigorated traditional forms in fields such as architecture and music. The decade following 1918 saw huge developments in English-language literature. We can consider James Joyce's* novel *Ulysses* (serialized in 1918; published as a book in 1922),T. S. Eliot's* long poem *The Waste Land* (1922), and the poet and novelist D. H. Lawrence's* *Lady Chatterley's Lover* (1928) to be landmark modernist texts. A crucial element of modernism, as Eliot argued in his important essay "Tradition and the Individual Talent" (1919), was its relationship to tradition and the literary canon.* This preoccupation was crucial to Woolf's thinking on a possible female canon in *A Room of One's Own*.[3]

> *"Have you any notion of how many books are written about women in the course of one year? Have you any notion how many are written by men? Are you aware that you are, perhaps, the most discussed animal in the universe?"*
>
> ──Virginia Woolf, *A Room of One's Own*

Overview of the Field

A Room of One's Own belongs to three different fields: it is simultaneously a feminist polemic (a controversial argument), an essay in literary theory, and a work of fiction. It draws on and responds to influences from each of these fields.

Feminism—often referred to as "The Women's Question"—was a key topic of debate in early twentieth-century Britain, and Woolf had precedents to draw on when considering the place of women writers in the world. In *A Vindication of the Rights of Woman* (1792) the pioneering feminist Mary Wollstonecraft had argued that a lack of education stood in the way of women's ability to be equal members of society.[4] The American feminist Margaret Fuller's* well-known 1843 work *Woman in the Nineteenth Century* also argued powerfully for women's rights to education and professional roles. In examining the relationship between women's economic circumstances and their ability to produce literature, Woolf was following in both women's footsteps.

A Room of One's Own also has precedents in literary theory and the development of fiction. T. S. Eliot's "Tradition and the Individual Talent" had helped crystalize modernism's fascination with past literary precedents: the "tradition". For Eliot, every writer must write from a deep knowledge of the great writers before him—an idea that became a mainstay of Anglo-American literary criticism from the 1930s onward.Woolf's contention that women writers need their own "forerunners" is part of this shift. Elements of modernism can also be seen in the form and style of *A Room*. A hybrid of essay and fiction, the piece's immersion in the consciousness and perception of its narrator is a hallmark of modernist narrative, and of Woolf's own novels.

Academic Influences

Though it is difficult to trace the direct influence of early feminist writers on *A Room of One's Own*, the essay is shaped by the feminist thought of its time. As the scholar Sowon Park of Oxford University has noted, many of its arguments were "very much in the air" thanks to writers such as the British actor and feminist Cicely Hamilton* and Charlotte Perkins Gilman* of the United States.[5] Anticipating Woolf's invention of "Judith Shakespeare" (a fictional sister for William Shakespeare),* Hamilton's 1909 *Marriage as a Trade* had debated why there were no female equivalents to Shakespeare.[6] Gilman, meanwhile, attacked the psychological effects of women's subjugation by men in her *The Man-Made World: Or, Our Androcentric Culture* (1911).[7]

More broadly, Woolf's influences came from the close circle of the Bloomsbury Group and the other artists with whom she associated. Through writing reviews, publishing at the Hogarth Press* (run by Woolf and her husband), and in personal interactions, she encountered the work of T. S. Eliot and James Joyce. The Bloomsbury Group itself was a melting pot for radical ideas and an experimental approach to art, thought, and sexuality—all of which can be traced in *A Room of One's Own*. Members of the group, such as economist John Maynard Keynes,* biographer Lytton Strachey,* art critic Clive Bell,* and painter Roger Fry,* were at the forefront of radical movements in their fields. Together they questioned the prevailing attitudes of the time, and their influence is pervasive in *A Room*, as in Woolf's work more generally.[8]

1 Michael H. Whitworth, *Virginia Woolf* (Oxford: Oxford University Press, 2005), 62.

2 Virginia Woolf, *A Room of One's Own* and *Three Guineas*, ed. Anna Snaith (Oxford: Oxford University Press, 2015), 74.

3 T. S. Eliot, "Tradition and the Individual Talent," in *Selected Essays* (London: Faber & Faber, 1951).

4 See Mary Wollstonecraft, *A Vindication of the Rights of Woman*, ed. Deidre Shauna Lynch (New York: W. W. Norton, 2009).

5 Sowon S. Park, "Suffrage and Virginia Woolf: 'The Mass Behind the Single Voice'," *The Review of English Studies* 56, no. 223 (2005): 122.

6 Cicely Hamilton, *Marriage as a Trade* (New York: Moffat, Yard and Co.,1909), chs. 14–16.

7 Charlotte Perkins Gilman, *The Man-Made World: Or, Our Androcentric Culture* (New York: Charlton, 1911).

8 There is an extensive bibliography on Bloomsbury: see Frances Spalding, *The Bloomsbury Group* (London: National Portrait Gallery, 2005); Rae Gallant Robbins, *The Bloomsbury Group: A Selective Bibliography*, 1st edn (Kenmore, WA: Price Guide Publishers, 1978); Heinz Antor, *The Bloomsbury Group: Its Philosophy, Aesthetics, and Literary Achievement* (Heidelberg: C. Winter, 1986).

MODULE 3
THE PROBLEM

KEY POINTS

- Virginia Woolf's essay examines two central questions: why are there so few female writers in the literary canon?* And what conditions are required for women to write great fiction?

- When Woolf was writing, the lack of famous female writers and artists through history was frequently cited as proof of women's intellectual inferiority.

- Woolf tackled this assumption by examining how social and material conditions through the ages had effectively silenced women writers.

Core Question

Virginia Woolf's *A Room of One's Own* was originally entitled "Women and Fiction" but, as Woolf states in its opening, the work deliberately leaves unanswered "the great problem of the true nature of woman and the true nature of fiction."[1] Instead, Woolf addressed two core questions: why are there so few women writers in the literary canon? And what conditions are required for women to produce great literature?

The first of these countered a key assumption of much antifeminist* rhetoric of the time: that women were less intelligent and able than men. The lack of famous female authors throughout history was frequently taken as evidence for such assumptions. Woolf, however, assumes equal intelligence and talent across the sexes, and asks instead what historical conditions had prevented women from becoming great writers. By seeking the real causes of the sparse feminine literary tradition, she was trying to counter the claim that women lacked literary ability.

The second core question related to the ongoing project of the women's movement* in Britain (a term often used for the struggle for women's suffrage* and for the early feminist* movement). Despite receiving full suffrage in 1928, just two months before the lectures that became *A Room of One's Own*, women were still subject to persistent inequalities and prejudices. Social expectations (such as those relating to education, marriage, and work), institutional bylaws (such as those preventing female students at the University of Cambridge* from being able to receive degrees until 1948), and material conditions (lack of money or privacy) still relegated women to a secondary position in British society. What changes, Woolf asked, would be necessary for women to be able to produce great literature, as men had throughout history?

> *"I thought how unpleasant it is to be locked out; and I thought how it is worse perhaps to be locked in; and thinking of the safety and prosperity of the one sex and the poverty and insecurity of the other and of the effect of tradition and of the lack of tradition upon the mind of a writer, I thought at last it was time to roll up the crumpled skin of the day."*
>
> ——Virginia Woolf, *A Room of One's Own*

The Participants

"The Women's Question" was the subject of heated debate in

Woolf's time. Even as women's legal rights were increased, social conventions lagged. As the South African novelist and feminist Olive Schreiner* noted in her 1911 book *Women and Labour*, women were "bound hand and foot ... by artificial constrictions and conventions, the remnants of a past condition of society."[2] Though World War I* had brought increased opportunities (and needs) for women to find work outside the domestic sphere, their progress beyond their traditional roles had caused an antifeminist and even misogynist*—"women-hating"—backlash.

In *A Room of One's Own*, Woolf caricatures this backlash in the fictional "Professor von X," and his "monumental work" entitled *The Mental, Moral, and Physical Inferiority of the Female Sex*.[3] Real antifeminists were hardly less extreme. In the late nineteenth century, the Harvard medical professor Edward Clarke* had suggested that a "masculine" education would physically damage women.[4] In Woolf's own time, the Austrian philosopher Otto Weininger's* *Sex and Character* (1903) stated that human characters were composed of the mixture of two "elements," the "male" and the "female"—the "female" only accounted for negative qualities.[5]

On the other side of the debate were pioneering feminists such as Olive Schreiner, Elizabeth Robins,* Eleanor Rathbone,* and Ray Strachey.*[6] Together with organizations such as the London Society for Women's Suffrage, Britain's first organization to campaign for women's right to vote on a national level, they were active in promoting both the campaign for full voting rights and a broader feminist outlook.

The Contemporary Debate

The debate on women's rights centered on the widespread assumption that women were either inferior to men or "naturally" different in ways which suited them to certain activities and excluded them from others. Clarke's *Sex in Education* (1873) is a good example of the latter position. Clarke's text was a touchstone for the pathology and medicalization of "Womanhood"—that is, for rendering femininity a diagnosable medical condition—and remained influential in the 1920s. "Man," Clarke stated, "is not superior to woman, nor woman to man," but there were "natural" differences, which could not be ignored.[7] Subjecting a girl to a "boy's [school] regimen," for instance, would end up "deranging the tides of her organization." Therefore, said Clarke, "identical education of the sexes is a crime before God and humanity."[8]

Otto Weininger was more straightforwardly misogynistic: the "female element" was purely negative, and any positive quality in a woman was a sign of "maleness." "All women who are truly famous and are of conspicuous mental ability," he wrote, possess "some of the anatomical characters of the male." Their maleness was the source of all their impressive qualities.[9] In regard to women and art, he was similarly direct: "there is no female genius... *and there never can be one*."[10] Such a thing would be "a contradiction in terms, for genius is simply intensified... universally conscious maleness."[11]

The women's movement itself was home to a range of opinions on women's rights and capabilities. But one common theme, as Schreiner argued, was that women had been unnaturally forced into a condition of "parasitism" (dependency on men) by social conditions and exclusions that made woman "the lesser sex" by robbing her "of all forms of active, conscious, social labour, and [reducing] her... to the passive exercise of her sex functions alone."[12]

1 Virginia Woolf, *A Room of One's Own* and *Three Guineas*, ed. Anna Snaith (Oxford: Oxford University Press, 2015), 4.

2 Olive Schreiner, *Woman and Labour* (London: T. Fisher Unwin, 1911), 24.

3 Woolf, *A Room of One's Own*, 24.

4 See Edward H. Clarke, *Sex in Education; or, A Fair Chance for Girls* (1873), in Nancy F. Cott, *Root of Bitterness: Documents of the Social History of American Women* (Lebanon, NH: University Press of New England, 1996), 331.

5 See Otto Weininger, *Sex and Character* (London: William Heinemann, 1906).

6 Sowon S. Park, "Suffrage and Virginia Woolf: 'The Mass Behind the Single Voice'," *The Review of English Studies* 56, no. 223 (2005): 122–3.

7 Clarke, *Sex in Education*, 330.

8 Clarke, *Sex in Education*, 331.

9 Weininger, *Sex and Character*, 65.

10 Weininger, *Sex and Character*, 189.

11 Weininger, *Sex and Character*, 189.

12 Schreiner, *Woman and Labour*, 78.

MODULE 4
THE AUTHOR'S CONTRIBUTION

KEY POINTS

* Virginia Woolf suggested that for women to produce great literature they needed to have a steady income and a private space of their own.

* Woolf's suggestion that material circumstances were vital to the production of literature reinforced the idea that women were no less intrinsically able to produce great writing than men, but had instead been prevented from doing so by their conditions.

* While Woolf was taking on ideas already in the main current of the women's movement* at the time, her approach to expressing them was deeply original.

Author's Aims

Virginia Woolf's *A Room of One's Own* grew out of two lectures given in October 1928 at Newnham College* and Girton College,* then the two women-only colleges of the University of Cambridge.* Returning from Cambridge after the Girton lecture, Woolf wrote in her diary that she "blandly told them to drink wine and have a room of their own"—a tired and joking comment that actually cuts to the heart of her aim to show how female writers could only achieve greatness under conditions of *material* equality with men.[1] That is to say, that while women had made some strides toward the full legal equality (such as voting rights and workplace equality) that had not been granted to them before, they were still materially worse off than men: they generally had less money, less comfortable lives, and less privacy.

Woolf aimed to show the negative impact these material inequalities had on women in general, and women writers in particular. In the final text of *A Room of One's Own*, Woolf comes to this central aim through four subsidiary aims: to show why there were so few female writers in the past; to show how this lack of a female literary tradition affected present-day women writers; to show the range of ways in which women found themselves literally and metaphorically locked into certain spaces (the home, for instance), and locked out of others (male-only institutions); and to show how the basic conditions of life affect people's consciousness and abilities.

Though many of these ideas were in the air at the time, Woolf's focus on the effects of material conditions on women through literature was deeply original. As the English literature scholar Laura Marcus suggests, *A Room of One's Own* remains perhaps "the most significant model for feminist* criticism" in the twentieth century.[2]

> *"But, you may say, we asked you to speak about women and fiction—what has that got to do with a room of one's own? I will try to explain."*
>
> ——Virginia Woolf, *A Room of One's Own*

Approach

Although the book grew out of lectures, *A Room of One's Own* is a complex mixture of essay and short fiction. The text begins in mid-sentence ("But, you may ask"), as if the reader has walked in, late, to a lecture. The narrator then goes on to say that she is going to use "all the liberties and licences of a novelist" to approach her subject. What follows is a fictional record of the narrator's experiences in Cambridge (dining at a male college and at a women's college) and in London (researching for the lecture, reading a contemporary female writer's novel), along with a thought experiment, in which the narrator imagines the possible life of a talented woman of Elizabethan* Britain (the Britain of Queen Elizabeth I, who reigned between 1558 and 1603).

Woolf chooses this original approach as a means of combining critical insights about female writers and their place in history with a first-hand account of her female experience as a writer. It allows her to access both the analytical logic and historical evidence of traditional literary criticism and the emotional resources of narrative fiction. It also means she can contribute to, and critically investigate, the "Women's Question" in a different mode from the impassioned political arguments of writers as Olive Schreiner.* Woolf encourages the reader's engagement with the narrator as a primary way of understanding and relating to her argument.

Another key element of Woolf's approach is her focus on the material conditions of life. The narrator's statement that having money "seemed infinitely more important" than having the vote has been controversial.[3] What it emphasizes, however, is Woolf's cultural-materialist* belief—the assumption that human capabilities are intimately related to their economic circumstances, and to even the smallest material aspects of life.

Contribution in Context

As Laura Marcus has noted, *A Room of One's Own* became a key text for feminists and feminist literary criticism in the second half of the twentieth century because of its forward-looking focus on personal rather than political issues.[4] However, as the scholars Sowon Park and Alex Zwerdling both point out, although *A Room* is original in many ways, it is also very much a product of Woolf's engagement with ideas that were already present in feminist writings.

Zwerdling notes that Woolf was "conscious of writing in a tradition that had begun over a century before with Mary Wollstonecraft's* *A Vindication of the Rights of Woman* and had continued well into her youth and adulthood."[5] Yet, at the same time, he points out, "her attitude toward the feminist legacy was essentially revisionist."[6] This was particularly the case in regard to the suffrage movement of Woolf's youth, which had become focused almost solely on the issue of women's votes in the belief that the other changes women desired would then follow. Woolf was openly skeptical about this, believing that "the psyche was much more resistant to change than the law." In other words, things would not really change until social attitudes and material conditions allowed women's and men's minds to see themselves and each other as equal.

Though the legal aspects of women's liberation were still an ongoing project, key rights had been won by 1928. Woolf, however, was more interested in the psychological and economic causes of continuing masculine domination. *A Room of One's Own* moved the focus of feminism back to a broader and more complex set of issues than just legal rights; a shift that should be seen as both part of a feminist tradition, and an original step in its immediate context.

1 Virginia Woolf, *A Writer's Diary*, ed. Leonard Woolf (London: Harcourt, 1954), 134.

2 Laura Marcus, *Virginia Woolf*, 2nd edn (Tavistock: Northcote House, 2004), 43.

3 Virginia Woolf, *A Room of One's Own* and *Three Guineas*, ed. Anna Snaith (Oxford: Oxford University Press, 2015), 29.

4 Marcus, *Virginia Woolf*, 41.

5 Alex Zwerdling, *Virginia Woolf and the Real World* (Berkeley: University of California Press, 1986), 211.

6 Zwerdling, *Woolf and the Real World*, 211.

SECTION 2
IDEAS

MAIN IDEAS

KEY POINTS

* The central theme of *A Room of One's Own* is that women throughout history have been prevented from fulfilling their potential by the economic and material disadvantages created by patriarchal* (male-dominated) society.

* Virginia Woolf argues that for women to write fiction—and enter into the literary canon*—they must have a steady income and private space.

* Woolf presents this idea through a fictional account of experience as a woman in the early twentieth century, and through an examination of women's lives and writing from the sixteenth century onwards.

Key Themes

The central theme of Virginia Woolf's *A Room of One's Own* is that, as Woolf states: "Intellectual freedom depends upon material things."[1] She sums this up in the memorable phrase that gives the essay its title "a woman must have money and a room of her own if she is to write fiction."[2] Even more precisely, she sets the figure at an income of £500 a year—the equivalent of just over £28,000 (more than $43,000) today.[3]

Woolf's demand is both literal and symbolic: these are real requirements as far as she is concerned, but they also represent larger things. The money "stands for the power to contemplate ... a lock on the door means the power to think for oneself."[4] Her main argument is that intellectual development, specifically talent for writing, is dependent not on a romantic notion of innate genius but on the most basic conditions of life: the food you eat, the clothes you wear, the spaces in which you can move or not move, how you are allowed and expected to act by social convention.

This idea lies behind the narrator's controversial notion that money and private space are more important than voting rights. To illustrate this, the narrator quotes the contemporary literary critic Sir Arthur Quiller-Couch,* stating "we may prate of democracy, but actually, a poor child in England has little more hope than the son of an Athenian slave to be emancipated into that intellectual freedom of which great writings are born."[5] For the narrator, her female contemporaries are like Quiller-Couch's poor child:"women have always been poor ... have had less intellectual freedom than the sons of Athenian slaves."[6] Even with the right to vote, the more important form of "intellectual emancipation" cannot be found without their economic and material circumstances improving.

> "[These] webs are not spun in mid-air by incorporeal creatures, but are the work of suffering human beings, and are attached to grossly material things, like health and money and the houses we live in."
>
> —— Virginia Woolf, *A Room of One's Own*

Exploring the Ideas

The central feature of Woolf's argument in *A Room of One's Own* is cultural materialism*: the idea that the characters, intellectual abilities, and beliefs of individuals are formed by the social structures and economic conditions of their world. This is to say, too, that the culture of a society—from popular songs through to newspapers, art, poetry, and fiction—is directly influenced by the "material conditions" of life in that society: how much individuals earn, the education they have access to, the houses they can afford to live in, the food they can afford to eat. This contrasts starkly with the common view that "art" is the product of extraordinary individuals whose minds are able, as Woolf puts it, "to rise above such things."[7] Believing that it is possible to do so, Woolf suggests, is to ignore the impact of everyday realities on the artist.

Alongside the cultural-materialist underpinning of Woolf's argument is the belief that great art comes from a tradition. This is a notion at the heart of the modernist* movement in literature, vocally put forward by Woolf's contemporaries Ezra Pound* and T. S. Eliot,* and expressed in the literary allusions of texts such as James Joyce's* celebrated novel *Ulysses*. In Woolf's words, "masterpieces are not single and solitary births; they are the outcome of many years of thinking in common, of thinking by the body of the people, so that the experience of the mass is behind the single voice."[8] In other words, all writers are dependent on their forerunners.

These ideas come together to explain the lack of women writers through history. First, male-dominated society—"patriarchy" in the standard feminist* terminology—has consistently deprived women of the economic independence and physical privacy necessary to allow them to write. Second, this has denied those rare women in a material position to write the female literary tradition necessary to help them create great literature. That there are so few great female writers, historically, is not evidence that women cannot write; it is only evidence that they have been prevented from writing by their social circumstances.

Language and Expression

Although *A Room of One's Own* is an accessible text, its form is intriguing. It combines aspects of critical writing and lectures with techniques from fiction—most notably Woolf's use of a narrator. Though written in the first person, with the narrator speaking as "I," Woolf makes clear that that "I" is not meant to be the author herself: "Here then was I (call me Mary Beton, Mary Seton, Mary Carmichael or by any name you please—it is not a matter of importance)."[9] Woolf uses the device to show that women in 1920s society are in no better a situation than their ancestors, and also that they are treated in many ways as identical and interchangeable by patriarchal society even though they are named individually. This is a central motif of her argument.The three names, taken from a sixteenth-century ballad, all appear elsewhere in the essay, as the narrator's aunt, as the principal of the fictional "Fernham" College, and as a female novelist. The device also allows Woolf to synthesize many elements of real, lived female experience and present them to the reader vividly, as though firsthand, through the fictional experience of the narrator.

Beyond its formal inventiveness, which shares much with Woolf's novels, *A Room of One's Own* makes as much use of humor and irony as it does of direct critical analysis of its subject.

Woolf's narrator openly satirizes the kind of male "authority" who writes misogynist* literature as if it were scientific fact. She presents a cutting portrait of "Professor X," imagined as "not in my picture a man attractive to women ... he had a great jowl ... very small eyes; he was very red in the face."[10] Elsewhere, writing of "all those great men" who have loved women across history (despite women's apparently clear inferiority) the narrator notes ironically that "all these relationships were absolutely Platonic [i.e., not sexual] I would not affirm."[11] A similar dry, sharp humor appears throughout the text.

1 Virginia Woolf, *A Room of One's Own* and *Three Guineas*, ed. Anna Snaith (Oxford: Oxford University Press, 2015), 81.

2 Woolf, *A Room of One's Own*, 3.

3 According to the Bank of England's inflation calculator: http://www. bankofengland.co.uk/education/ Pages/resources/inflationtools/calculator/ flash/default.aspx, accessed August 5, 2015.

4 Woolf, *A Room of One's Own*, 80.

5 Woolf, *A Room of One's Own*, 81; original source Arthur Quiller-Couch, *On the Art of Writing* (New York: G. P. Putnam's Sons, 1916), 39.

6 Woolf, *A Room of One's Own*, 81.

7 Woolf, *A Room of One's Own*, 81.

8 Woolf, *A Room of One's Own*, 49.

9 Woolf, *A Room of One's Own*, 4.

10 Woolf, *A Room of One's Own*, 24.

11 Woolf, *A Room of One's Own*, 65.

MODULE 6
SECONDARY IDEAS

KEY POINTS

- The two key secondary ideas of *A Room of One's Own* are that it might be possible to imagine or uncover a hidden female literary canon* and that writing has a close, complex relationship with gender.

- The first of these ideas underpins the argument that women throughout history have been prevented from writing by their circumstances; the second allows Virginia Woolf to question what a female canon would or should look like.

- The alternative women's history of literature has proved extremely influential for later feminist* literary criticism.

Other Ideas

One of the most influential aspects of Virginia Woolf's *A Room of One's Own* is Woolf's thought experiment on "Judith Shakespeare." A fictional sister to William Shakespeare,* Woolf's Judith illustrates the ways in which women's voices have been silenced or suppressed throughout history. As Woolf notes, this suppression is neither simple nor deliberate. It is complex and indirect: Judith's father discourages her from reading precisely because he loves her, and does not want her to suffer social exclusion.[1] Like her brother, she escapes to London to follow her dream of writing and acting. But unlike William, she is laughed at and excluded, and eventually, pregnant with an illegitimate baby, she kills herself.[2] Woolf uses this imagined life to interrogate how and why history presents so few examples of female writers.

Moving on from "Judith Shakespeare," Woolf's narrator charts the few women writers in English who constitute the sparse "female tradition" in literature: Aphra Behn,* the Brontë* sisters, Jane Austen,* George Eliot.* Women's "creative power," the narrator initially suggests, "differs greatly from the creative power of men," and women's writing should reflect that difference.[3] Later, however, the narrator asks herself whether or not writing should be gendered in this way. If there are "two sexes in the mind corresponding to the two sexes in the body" might they "also require to be united in order to get complete satisfaction and happiness," so that they may create great literature?[4] If so, does such a union undo the idea of "female writing" or a possible "female canon"?

> "Let me imagine that Shakespeare had a wonderfully gifted sister, called Judith, let us say ... She was as adventurous, as imaginative, as agog to see the world as he was. But she was not sent to school."
>
> —— Virginia Woolf, *A Room of One's Own*

Exploring the Ideas

"Judith Shakespeare" is central to the argument in *A Room of One's Own* about the suppression of women's voices. The invention of a female counterpart to the greatest writer in English history is used by Woolf to illustrate that, regardless of her natural talents, a woman in Shakespeare's time could never have become "Shakespeare." "Judith" also illustrates the complex and indirect nature of women's suppression: she is not silenced deliberately, or out of conscious hatred by men, but by social conditions. She "was the apple of her father's eye," and "Nick Greene ... took pity on her"; the men in her life act with good intentions, but within a context that can only lead to Judith's subjugation and silencing.[5] Woolf extends this to say that it was impossible for a real sixteenth-century woman to have "Shakespeare's genius," as genius "is not born among laboring, uneducated, servile people," and such was the condition of women at the time.[6]

While *A Room of One's Own* attacks deliberate misogyny*— the "anger disguised and complex" behind Professor X's hatred, for instance—Judith's suppression emphasizes the widespread nature of male-dominated society's unconscious, unintended, subjugation of women. Elsewhere Woolf expresses this in the ironically polite figure that prevents the narrator from entering the library in the all-male college she visits. He is "a guardian angel," "a deprecating, silvery kindly gentleman" who "regretted" that women cannot enter the library without a college fellow, or a letter of introduction.[7]

This view provides Woolf with a way to imagine what has been lost through women's "infinitely obscure lives," to imagine a continuous forced silence beneath the noise of male history.[8] This is one of the text's most enduring contributions to feminist literary criticism, with Woolf asking the reader to imagine the possibilities disguised by that silence: "When ... one reads of a witch being ducked, or a woman possessed by devils, of a wise woman selling herbs ... then I think we are on the track of a lost novelist, a suppressed poet, of some mute and inglorious Jane Austen."[9]

This muteness still leaves open, for Woolf, the question of what a true "women's fiction" would resemble—a question which leads directly to one of the essay's less-discussed ideas: literary androgyny.*

Overlooked

In a text as brief and influential as *A Room of One's Own* it is hard to talk of overlooked ideas, but the narrator's thoughts on whether writing can or should be "gendered" (i.e. male or female) remain more ambiguous and puzzling than the central claims of the essay. These ideas are occasionally sidelined in discussions of the text. Importantly, though, they make possible a lesbian reading of the work, placing *A Room* as an early "queer"* text (i.e. a text in the recently named theoretical and cultural current of inquiry into identities outside the heterosexual "norm") as well as an early feminist text.

In chapter 5, the narrator argues that a "women's fiction" can only come out of a female tradition, because women's "creative power differs greatly" from men's.[10] Later, she questions this idea. Seeing a couple getting into a London taxi together makes her wonder "whether there are two sexes in the mind" as well as in the body, and whether they must be balanced together for "complete satisfaction and happiness" in literature, as in life.[11] If so, should there be such a thing as "female" writing, or should all writers be "androgynous"—simultaneously male and female?

The idea of the "man-womanly" or "woman-manly" mind, of the coexistence of "female" and "male" elements, was a common

116

theme of contemporary theories on sex—including, notably, the Austrian philosopher Otto Weininger's misogynist work *Sex and Character*, with which Woolf was familiar.[12] "Androgyny" was frequently associated with homosexuality—as in Weininger's presumption that the Classical lesbian poet Sappho* (circa 630–570 B.C.E.) was more male than female.[13] Woolf was aware that readers might see a lesbian subtext in *A Room of One's Own,* writing in her diary before the essay's publication that she would be "hinted at for a Sapphist" (i.e. a lesbian).[14] Though it remains only the hint of a theme in the essay itself, lesbianism was an important aspect of Woolf's own sexuality. Her 1928 novel *Orlando*, about a character who changes sex over the course of an unnaturally long life, was, as Laura Marcus notes, "a very public 'love-letter'" to her then lover Vita Sackville-West.*[15] As such, the brief reflection on literary "androgyny" represents an important gesture not just toward "women's writing" but also toward what would come to be known as "queer writing."

---

1 Virginia Woolf, *A Room of One's Own* and *Three Guineas*, ed. Anna Snaith (Oxford: Oxford University Press, 2015), 36.

2 Woolf, *A Room of One's Own*, 36–7.

3 Woolf, *A Room of One's Own*, 66.

4 Woolf, *A Room of One's Own*, 74.

5 Woolf, *A Room of One's Own*, 36, 37.

6 Woolf, *A Room of One's Own*, 37.

7 Woolf, *A Room of One's Own*, 6.

8 Woolf, *A Room of One's Own*, 67.

9 Woolf, *A Room of One's Own*, 37.

10 Woolf, *A Room of One's Own*, 66.

11 Woolf, *A Room of One's Own*, 74.

12 Otto Weininger, *Sex and Character* (London: William Heinemann, 1906).

13 Weininger, *Sex and Character*, 66.

14 Virginia Woolf, *A Writer's Diary*, ed. Leonard Woolf (London: Harcourt, 1954), 148.

15 Laura Marcus, *Virginia Woolf*, 2nd edn (Tavistock: Northcote House, 2004), 55.

MODULE 7
ACHIEVEMENT

KEY POINTS

* Virginia Woolf's *A Room of One's Own* was popular with contemporary readers and went on to influence generations of feminists.*

* The critical success of Woolf's novels helped the essay find a wide audience, and gave extra credibility to Woolf's arguments.

* While *A Room* remains a powerful text with potential applications in other contexts, its main limitation is that its arguments are specific to 1920s Britain.

Assessing the Argument

One important early reviewer of Virginia Woolf's *A Room of One's Own*, the critic and novelist Arnold Bennett,* was quick to note that it has, at heart, a very simple "thesis"—that you must have £500 a year and a room with a lock on the door if you are going to write fiction or poetry. To Bennett, this was at best "disputable."[1] For Bennett, the great Russian novelist Fyodor Dostoevsky* and he himself were counterexamples. What Bennett's review misses, however, is the broader drift of Woolf's argument that "intellectual freedom depends on material things," and that women throughout history have been materially much worse off than men.[2] She vividly evokes not only how these material disadvantages were felt in earlier times, but also, through the use of a narrator, how they are felt in her own time. As a result, *A Room* makes a strong case for the fundamental argument that lies behind Woolf's apparently glib premise.

Beyond this thesis, however, *A Room of One's Own* is hard to pin down. In Bennett's unsympathetic analysis, it is undisciplined and full of "padding," because Woolf "talks about everything but the thesis."[3] In a sense this is true: Woolf opens up many lines of argument and approaches the core questions of "women and fiction" from several angles, deliberately avoiding clear conclusions. This, though, is crucial to the essay's mode of inquiry, and to the complex issues it examines. In the opening paragraph— before the narrator takes the stage—Woolf refers to the money and the room as a "minor point."[4] By implication, the major points of the text are its "unsolved problems"—"the true nature of woman and the true nature of fiction."[5] Remaining open-ended on these topics is crucial to the essay, and one reason why its arguments continue to have implications for readers today.

> *"[When] I ask you to write more books I am urging you to do what will be for your good and for the good of the world at large."*
>
> —— Virginia Woolf, *A Room of One's Own*

Achievement in Context

Though Woolf was already a literary success when *A Room of One's Own* was published in 1929, the essay helped establish her reputation as one of the brightest literary stars of her time. Since 1925 she had published three novels that established her as one of Britain's most important novelists: *Mrs Dalloway* (1925), *To the Lighthouse* (1927), and *Orlando* (1928). In 1927 her yearly income from her novels was just over £500. After *Orlando,* her earnings from her books came to nearly three times as much.[6] When *A Room* was published, it received positive reviews and sold faster than any of her previous books.[7] In England, the Hogarth Press* (run by Woolf and her husband, Leonard) printed 14,650 copies in the first six months after publication.[8]

A Room of One's Own has gone on to be an important text not just for Woolf studies, but in a number of different disciplines: women's studies, gender studies, queer* studies, literary theory, and feminist studies. As the Woolf scholar and feminist literary theorist Susan Gubar* points out, it has come to be "a classic— if not *the* touchstone text—in the history of feminism."[9] A crucial aspect of the text's success, as the scholar Alex Zwerdling notes, is that Woolf was able with her novelist's "powers of observation and divination to probe depths the earlier feminist writers had left largely unplumbed."[10] This allowed her, in the wake of women winning the right to vote in 1928, "to restore a sense of the complexity of the issues after the radical simplification that had seemed necessary for political action."[11] In other words, *A Room*, with its complex mixture of fiction, literary criticism, and historical analysis, shone a light on issues and problems that had otherwise been left in the dark.

Limitations

While many of the issues raised by Woolf in *A Room of One's Own* remain relevant to feminism and literary criticism today, the text is very much a product of its time. Although Woolf is sensitive to and critical of the ways in which society has silenced women throughout history, *A Room* is not interested in history's other silenced and suppressed groups. Writing as part of the white upper class in early twentieth-century Britain, Woolf tackles the plight of women, but has blind spots when it comes to women of other colors and classes.

Woolf's essay is deeply concerned with the importance of material things and economic security. But her implied audience is women who, though disadvantaged by their sex, were largely members of the privileged upper classes. Woolf was part of a class where the possibility of being left an inheritance of £500 a year, like the essay's narrator, was real.Women of the working classes were not so fortunate, suffering subjugation both as women and as members of Britain's "lower classes." Woolf addresses herself to women who, like her, did not need to fear destitution, even if they were not in control of their own voices and destinies.

While Woolf's model of listening for the voices of the silenced has proved relevant to contexts in which race is central, another blind spot is that of color. The black American author and activist Alice Walker,* in her essay "In Search of Our Mothers' Gardens," critiques Woolf's lack of interest in nonwhite women. As the title of the essay suggests, Walker is interested, like Woolf, in a female tradition—her "mother's"—but hers is specifically an African American female tradition. Her "mothers" are women who, like the early African American poet Phillis Wheatley* (1753–84), were slaves. Like her white counterparts in the eighteenth century, Wheatley could not hope to have access to £500 and a room of her own, but her suppression went further than theirs: as a slave, she "owned not even herself."[12] Walker's essay seeks out the silenced black women around Wheatley, constructing her own alternative history of the voices suppressed by colonial society.

1 See Arnold Bennett, "Queen of the High-Brows" (review of *A Room of One's Own*, *Evening Standard*, November 28, 1929), in *Virginia Woolf: The Critical Heritage*, ed. Robin Majumdar and Allen McLaurin (London: Routledge, 1975), 259.

2 Virginia Woolf, *A Room of One's Own* and *Three Guineas*, ed. Anna Snaith (Oxford: Oxford University Press, 2015), 81.

3 Bennett, "Queen of the High-Brows," 259.

4 Woolf, *A Room of One's Own*, 3.

5 Woolf, *A Room of One's Own*, 3.

6 Hermione Lee, *Virginia Woolf* (London: Vintage, 1997), 558.

7 Julia Briggs, *Virginia Woolf: An Inner Life* (Orlando: Harcourt, 2005), 235.

8 See "Note on the Text," in Woolf, *A Room of One's Own*, xxxvii.

9 Susan Gubar, "Introduction," in Virginia Woolf, *A Room of One's Own*, ed. Susan Gubar (Orlando: Harcourt, 2005), xxxvi.

10 Alex Zwerdling, *Virginia Woolf and the Real World* (Berkeley: University of California Press, 1986), 216.

11 Zwerdling, *Woolf and the Real World*, 217.

12 Alice Walker, *In Search of Our Mothers' Gardens: Womanist Prose* (London: Phoenix, 2005), 235.

PLACE IN THE AUTHOR'S WORK

KEY POINTS

* Virginia Woolf was a prolific writer of both fiction and criticism, best known for her focus on the fine detail of human experience.

* Although *A Room of One's Own* is a short text in a productive career, it was a success in its own time, and remains Woolf's best-known critical work.

* Woolf's reputation rests, ultimately, on her novels, which rank among the most highly regarded works of twentieth-century literature; she is perhaps best known today for *To the Lighthouse* (1925) and *Mrs Dalloway* (1927).

Positioning

A Room of One's Own is only one text in Virginia Woolf's large and varied body of work. Woolf was prolific across several genres: in addition to nine novels published between 1915 and 1937, and *Between the Acts* published in 1941 after her suicide, she wrote short stories, essays, and book reviews. Her collected essays alone run to six volumes. Her reputation has continued to grow since her death, and she is considered to be one of the most significant writers of the twentieth century, a key figure in the histories of the novel, of modernism,* and of women's writing.

In her career before *A Room of One's Own*, Woolf had already distinguished herself as a novelist concerned with the fine detail of human experience, and the psychological effects of the world on the individual. *The Voyage Out* (1915) tells of a young woman on a journey to South America, and her intellectual awakening through contact with other passengers on the boat. *Night and Day* (1919), which touches on the campaign for women's votes, linked the social challenges facing modern women to the idolizing of the past's "great men."

It is the novels of the 1920s, however, that remain Woolf's most widely recognized and studied: *Jacob's Room* (1922), *Mrs Dalloway* (1925), and *To the Lighthouse* (1927). All three explore the links and interactions between individual and collective experience, shaped by the characters' location in a nation, city, and family. In 1928, Woolf published *Orlando: A Biography*, which satirized traditional biography by presenting the life of a fantastical multi-gendered protagonist who lives for hundreds of years.

In *A Room of One's Own,* Woolf speaks with the critical authority of the established writer.The text explores feminist* themes she would examine again in later works such as the essay "Professions for Women" (1931) and *Three Guineas* (1938). Touching on themes central to her fiction and later critical texts, *A Room* is a key part of her output.

> "I am by no means confining you to fiction. If you would please me—and there are thousands like me—you would write books of travel and adventure, and research and scholarship, and history and biography, and criticism and philosophy and science. By so doing you will certainly profit the art of fiction. For books have a way of influencing each other."
>
> ——Virginia Woolf, *A Room of One's Own*

Integration

A Room of One's Own addresses issues through fiction, and through a narrative telling of lived experience. This is the most evident point it has in common with Woolf's other work. In her novels, particularly from the 1920s onward, Woolf evolved a modernist stream-of-consciousness* technique, according to which the narrative voice is more fluid than earlier styles, such as the traditional omniscient narrator of many Victorian novels, and the reader is allowed to "see" the events of the novel from the perspective of a character or characters. In Woolf's work, characters' inner lives (their thoughts, emotions, memories) are vividly detailed as they experience external events, or interact with one another.

In trading the traditional voice of the lecturer—who, Woolf states, would provide "a nugget of pure truth"—for that of the fictive narrator, Woolf draws an important link between *A Room of One's Own* and her novels. The essay's readers are asked to interpret the text in the same way they might read *Mrs Dalloway* or *To the Lighthouse*: "Lies will flow from my lips," Woolf tells them, "but there may perhaps be some truth mixed up with them; it is for you to seek out this truth."[1] Readers are, in other words, encouraged to engage with the text actively, not as passive "listeners" at a lecture.

A Room of One's Own is also thematically consistent with Woolf's body of work as a whole. Critically, she would revisit feminism in the longer essay *Three Guineas* (1938), but she also addressed suffrage* and the women's movement* in general in her fiction, both before and after 1929. In *Night and Day* (1919), the character Mary Datchet is a suffrage activist, responsible for the paperwork, pamphlets, and discussion groups of a women's rights organization. In *The Years* (1937), Rose Pargiter is a "suffragette,"* involved with less peaceful activism for the vote.[2]

Significance

A Room of One's Own remains a significant work in at least two different areas. In Woolf studies, it is seen as the text that most clearly details Woolf's intellectual relationship to the issues at the heart of feminism. Though it makes use of fictional narrative techniques, it continues to be read as a more direct statement than anything dealing with the women's movement found in her novels. But Woolf's reputation as one of English literature's most important figures does not rest on *A Room*. That role is filled by the landmark novels she produced. While *A Room* remains an important text for those trying to understand Woolf's views on feminism, and is often read as a means of placing her in context as an early twentieth-century female author, it is a minor work relative to her output as a whole.

However, this does not prevent *A Room of One's Own* from being a key text in literary and feminist history. In shifting emphasis from legal rights for women to broader social and psychological issues—above all the mental impact of patriarchy* on individual women—the essay anticipated the major developments in feminist thought in the second half of the twentieth century. While the women's movement of Woolf's lifetime (which has subsequently come to be known as first-wave feminism)* concentrated on gaining legal and political victories, the second-wave feminism* of the period after World War II* shifted focus to the kinds of psychological and cultural issues examined by Woolf's essay. Some critics have suggested that *A Room* has been co-opted to views that Woolf might not agree with. But there is no doubt that, as Laura Marcus observes, it is the text through which Woolf "was granted centre stage" in debates about feminism, women, and literature.[3]

---

1 Virginia Woolf, *A Room of One's Own* and *Three Guineas*, ed. Anna Snaith (Oxford: Oxford University Press, 2015), 4.

2 For an extended examination of Woolf's relationship to the women's movement, see Sowon S. Park, "Suffrage and Virginia Woolf: 'The Mass Behind the Single Voice'," *Review of English Studies* 56, no. 223 (2005): 119–34.

3 Laura Marcus, *Virginia Woolf*, 2nd edn (Tavistock: Northcote House, 2004), 41.

SECTION 3
IMPACT

THE FIRST RESPONSES

KEY POINTS

* On its publication, the main criticisms of *A Room of One's Own* were that its main point was disputable, and that Virginia Woolf's indirect writing style distracted from the central arguments.

* Woolf did not respond to her critics, though the more direct feminist* essay *Three Guineas* (1938) can be seen as a sequel to *A Room*.

* Since its original publication, Woolf's literary stature has encouraged readers to take the essay on its own terms, and it is now seen as a key moment in feminist literary history.

Criticism

On its publication in 1929, Virginia Woolf's *A Room of One's Own* received a relatively limited critical response. Before publication, Woolf herself was worried that the essay's combination of fiction and critical writing, along with its indirect approach to its central questions, would not "be taken seriously."[1] Expecting a condescending critical response from male reviewers, she thought she might be praised for her style and her "very feminine logic," and that they might recommend it as "a book to be put in the hands of girls."[2]

Reality was close to Woolf's predictions. An anonymous review in the important literary paper the *Times Literary Supplement* praised the essay as "delightfully peripatetic," meaning that it wandered in subject matter, "spirited and goodtempered [*sic*]."[3] The prominent literary critic and novelist Arnold Bennett* was similarly condescending. While praising Woolf's style—"she can write"—he said the indirectness of the essay was accidental. Woolf could not stick to her point because she was a "victim of her extraordinary gift of fancy."[4] The essay's "thesis"—that one must have £500 a year and a room with a lock on the door to write fiction—was "disputable," however.[5] To prove that, he offered himself and the Russian novelist Fyodor Dostoyevsky* as examples of writers with neither money nor room, ignoring the text's broader questions about women.

Despite this, *A Room of One's Own* was critically praised. One contemporary critic anticipated later feminist readings of the essay by stating that "Woolf's attitude is far from the polemics of traditional feminism. From the ashes of those bitter conflicts has risen a new conception of the whole problem, to which Mrs Woolf gives a form and a voice."[6] That form and voice would go on to define later feminist readings of the essay.

> "I shall get no criticism, except of the evasive jocular kind ... the press will be kind and talk of its charm and sprightliness; also I shall be attacked for a feminist and hinted at for a Sapphist ... I shall get a good many letters from young women. I am afraid it will not be taken seriously. Mrs. Woolf is so accomplished a writer that all she says makes easy reading."
>
> —— Virginia Woolf, *A Writer's Diary*

Responses

Though Woolf was partially correct in her predictions of patronizing reviews, above all by Arnold Bennett, *A Room of One's Own* sold extremely well. It was, in fact, Woolf's biggest-selling book to date, and its sales helped cement her financial independence as well as her literary reputation.[7] After publication, Woolf did not respond to the critics or engage in dialogue with them. She let the book make its own arguments.

In a sense, however, Woolf had already responded to possible negative criticism before the essay's publication. The drafts of the book show how sensitive Woolf was to potential criticism, to her audience, and to how her writing might reflect on herself. Adapting the lectures upon which it was originally based, she toned down some harsh claims, removed negative references to particular authors, and created an alter ego (another version of herself) to be the narrator for her text. She was, as the author and literature scholar Susan Gubar* notes, "worried about sounding strident," and about being "rejected as either a feminist or a lesbian," and took steps to ensure this would not be the case.[8] These alterations give the essay its elusive and playful indirectness, and also a great deal of its richness.

Later responses have tended to praise *A Room* precisely *for* its feminism and its lesbian subtext, and its elusiveness has only helped broaden the number of interpretations that seem valid. As Gubar states, it is now "a classic—if not *the* touchstone text—in the history of feminism," heavily anticipating the psychological, social, economic, and ideological concerns at the center of second-wave feminism.*[9]

Conflict and Consensus

A Room of One's Own remains a text that generates a great deal of debate within Woolf studies, feminist literary theory, and feminism more generally.Though it is accepted as "undoubtedly Woolf's most important contribution to literary criticism and theory," and a key text in the history of feminist thought, debates still continue over precisely what Woolf intended to say, and over whether or not that might provide a model for thought in a contemporary context.[10] As Laura Marcus notes: "It is striking that Woolf has been used by so many different critics to exemplify one or another of a variety of incommensurate positions and that such weight has been attached to establishing her commitment to whichever position she is held to represent."[11]

Woolf returned to her own views on feminist issues in her 1938 work *Three Guineas*, initially conceived as a sequel to *A Room of One's Own*. Published a decade after the earlier essay, *Three Guineas* again examines the distance between women's apparent legal rights and what their material conditions actually allow them to achieve. The focus this time, however, shifts away from creative expression and art toward political agency (freedom). *A Room of One's Own* criticized the psychological effects of patriarchy* on women. Returning to that theme, *Three Guineas* more directly emphasizes the need for women to have visible, active, equal roles in society. Close to the outbreak of World War II,* *Three Guineas* also makes a direct link between patriarchy and wasteful conflict—a stronger direct political message than anything to be found in *A Room*.

Despite the more precise tone of *Three Guineas*, however, *A Room of One's Own* remains the key text for considering Woolf's views on and contribution to feminism. As such, it continues to be a subject of debate and of reappropriation by new generations of feminist thinkers.

---

1 Virginia Woolf, *A Writer's Diary*, ed. Leonard Woolf (London: Harcourt, 1954), 148.

2 Woolf, *Writer's Diary*, 148.

3 See Robin Majumdar and Allen McLaurin, eds., *Virginia Woolf: The Critical Heritage* (London: Routledge & Kegan Paul, 1975), 255, 256.

4 Majumdar and McLaurin, eds., *Virginia Woolf: The Critical Heritage*, 258, 259.

5 Majumdar and McLaurin, eds., *Virginia Woolf: The Critical Heritage*, 259.

6 Majumdar and McLaurin, eds., *Virginia Woolf: The Critical Heritage*, 260.

7 Hermione Lee, *Virginia Woolf* (London: Vintage 1997), 557.

8 See Susan Gubar, "Introduction," in Virginia Woolf, *A Room of One's Own,* ed. Susan Gubar (Orlando: Harcourt, 2005), xxxvii. See also Virginia Woolf, *Women & Fiction: The Manuscript Versions of A Room of One's Own*, ed. S. P. Rosenbaum (Oxford: Blackwell, 1992).

9 Gubar, "Introduction," xxxvi.

10 Jane Goldman, *The Cambridge Introduction to Virginia Woolf* (Cambridge: Cambridge University Press, 2006), 97.

11 Laura Marcus, *Virginia Woolf*, 2nd edn (Tavistock: Northcote House, 2004), 41.

MODULE 10
THE EVOLVING DEBATE

KEY POINTS

* With the rise of second-wave feminism* in the postwar* period, a movement that addressed the wider civic and cultural status of women, Virginia Woolf's central argument that the material conditions of life have a huge effect on women's ability to produce art was widely accepted.

* Though second-wave feminism had many influences, *A Room of One's Own* can be seen as an important precursor to many of its ideas and debates.

* Woolf's arguments in the essay have been applied in new contexts in recent years, proving that it has relevance to areas Woolf herself did not foresee.

Uses and Problems

Virginia Woolf's *A Room of One's Own* has a presence in feminist* literary theory that is both controversial and influential. The period after World War II* saw the emergence of what has come to be known as second-wave feminism. In contrast to the first-wave feminism* of Woolf's own time, which concentrated on the winning of legal rights and entry into university and the professions, second-wave feminism had broader concerns that had much in common with Woolf's arguments and questions in *A Room*.

Among the concerns of second-wave feminism, the widespread and negative influence of patriarchy* is central. Woolf's vivid characterization in *A Room of One's Own* of England's top-tobottom privileging of men, and locking out of women, was bound to strike a chord. So too, as French feminism in particular became increasingly concerned with society as a "textual"* (i.e. readable) set of symbols and languages, was Woolf's concern with feminine traditions and textuality. In particular, the statement in *A Room* that "it would be a thousand pities if women wrote like men" (though contradicted later in the essay),[1] anticipated one of the major themes of 1970s and 1980s feminist theory—Hélène Cixous's* *écriture féminine*, or "feminine writing."[2]

At the same time, however, changes and developments in feminist thought provided a critique of *A Room of One's Own*, most notably from the American feminist literary critic Elaine Showalter.* Showalter framed her *A Literature of Their Own* (1977) as a long response to what she saw as Woolf's shortcomings. It would not be until the 1980s that influential figures such as the Norwegian literary theorist Toril Moi* would restore Woolf's reputation.

> "It is not of course surprising that many male critics have found Woolf a frivolous Bohemian* and negligible Bloomsbury* aesthete, but the rejection of this great feminist writer by so many of her Anglo-American feminist daughters requires further explanation."
>
> Toril Moi, *Sexual/Textual Politics*

Schools of Thought

As the feminist literary scholar Jane Goldman notes, in the 1970s *A Room of One's Own* became a recurrent point of reference in debates on the theoretical aspects of feminism. In particular, the essay's cultural materialist* take on women's suppression—examining it through the effects of everyday life and economic circumstances—was taken on by Marxist feminists who, having identified the ways in which women are oppressed by the workings of the social and economic system of capitalism, saw it as powerful proof of the relevance of Marxist theory to women's situations.[3] Such readings were confirmed within Woolf studies by Jane Marcus's *Art and Anger: Reading Like a Woman* (1988) and *Virginia Woolf and the Languages of Patriarchy* (1987).

As Showalter's *A Literature of Their Own* showed, however, it was also possible for feminists to disagree with Woolf, even to the point of attacking her as unfeminist. For Showalter, by questioning whether or not a specifically "female" way of writing is a worthy goal, Woolf is guilty of a "flight into androgyny"—of seeking to not be a woman, and therefore not be a feminist either.[4] Rather than paving the way for the liberation of authentic female voices, *A Room of One's Own* is, for Showalter, a text that leads women into "the sphere of exile and the eunuch"—a place outside of society, where they will be deprived of their sex.[5]

While Showalter's critique struck a chord with feminists wanting to define a specifically female identity through history, it soon came under attack. It was definitively countered by influential theorist Toril Moi—who promotes a more flexible conception of "woman" and women's voices in her work—in her 1985 book *Textual/Sexual Politics*. As Moi suggested, with some tact, if feminist theorists could not find a way of using "the work of the greatest British woman writer of [the twentieth] century," then "the fault may lie with their own critical and theoretical perspectives."[6]

In Current Scholarship

A Room of One's Own remains a key text in Woolf studies, and a seminal work in the history of literary theory and feminism. This does not mean, however, that a simple consensus has been reached about its meaning. Woolf's strategy of speaking through a narrator, and of withholding commitment to any clear "message" beyond the need for women to have money and privacy, has left the essay open to many different interpretations—often contradictory. As the author and scholar Susan Gubar* notes, critics have at different times labeled it as both feminist and antifeminist*—"too angry in [its] caricaturing of men" and "fearful of rage"; "quasi-Marxist" and "elitist."[7] Such contradictions show the place of *A Room* in many critical debates, all of which stem from its complex and challenging prose, as well as differing attitudes toward its author and the context of its creation.

Toril Moi's restoration of Woolf within feminist literary theory left open a path for other feminist theorists to follow, ensuring a place for *A Room of One's Own* in literary and feminist studies ever since. Two books in particular continue to mark the field: the literary studies professor Makiko Minow-Pinkney's *Virginia Woolf and the Problem of the Subject* (1987), and the English Literature professor Rachel Bowlby's* *Virginia Woolf: Feminist Destinations* (1988; republished with five further essays in 1997).[8] The former brought Woolf together with French feminist theory; the latter uses psychoanalytical* readings of Woolf's feminism to make a case for her work's open and shifting meanings.

Since the 1990s, with the rise of lesbian feminist perspectives and queer* theory in literary studies, *A Room of One's Own* continues to be read and discussed, perhaps more than ever before. Recent readings of the essay, and of Woolf's work more generally, have been marked by sustained examinations of her fluid sexuality, with Eileen Barrett and Patricia Cramer's collection *Virginia Woolf: Lesbian Readings* (1997) remaining influential.

1 Virginia Woolf, *A Room of One's Own* and *Three Guineas*, Anna Snaith (Oxford: Oxford University Press, 2015), 66.

2 See Hélène Cixous, "The Laugh of the Medusa," trans. Keith and Paula Cohen, *Signs* 1, no. 4 (1976): 875–93.

3 Jane Goldman, *The Cambridge Introduction to Virginia Woolf* (Cambridge: Cambridge University Press, 2006), 130. See also Virginia Woolf, *Women and Writing,* ed. Michèle Barrett (London: Women's Press, 1979).

4 Elaine Showalter, *A Literature of Their Own: From Charlotte Brontë to Doris Lessing* (Princeton: Princeton University Press, 1999), 263.

5 Showalter, *A Literature of Their Own*, 285.

6 Toril Moi, *Textual/Sexual Politics: Feminist Literary Theory*, 2nd edn (London: Routledge, 2002), 9.

7 Woolf, *A Room of One's Own*, viii.

8 Makiko Minow-Pinkney, *Virginia Woolf and the Problem of the Subject* (Edinburgh: Edinburgh University Press, 2010); Rachel Bowlby, *Feminist Destinations and Further Essays on Virginia Woolf* (Oxford: Blackwell, 1997).

MODULE 11
IMPACT AND INFLUENCE TODAY

KEY POINTS

- *A Room of One's Own* remains an essential text in Woolf studies and in the history of feminism.*

- It is a persuasive work on the deep consequences of daily social exclusion and material disadvantage, challenging readers to consider their own lived experience in regard to feminism.

- Its suggestive questioning of the role of social and material conditions in shaping women's lives and creative work remains relevant today, even if social and material conditions have changed considerably.

Position

There can be no doubt that Virginia Woolf's *A Room of One's Own* remains a key text for students of literature. Woolf's position as, in the literary theorist Toril Moi's* words, "the greatest British woman writer of [the twentieth] century" has helped maintain the essay's place in the literary canon.* It is a seminal text in the development of Woolf's own career, in British modernism,* and in feminist literary theory. Even where theorists, such as the influential feminist scholar Elaine Showalter,* have disagreed with Woolf's approach and suggestions, the essay is a landmark in the history of women's literature.

A crucial element in *A Room*'s continuing presence in critical debate is its rich and complex nature. An open-ended text beyond its deceptively simple thesis, it continues to draw scholarly exploration and revisions. Both formally and in terms of its themes, it also remains influential. The American feminist literary critic Susan Gubar's* *Rooms of Our Own* (2006) is only one of a number of contemporary critical texts that either make direct references to Woolf's essay or take stylistic and intellectual inspiration from Woolf's original.[1] Within literary and feminist studies, Woolf remains a crucial figure, and, though *A Room* is only a single slim essay among her prolific output, it remains one of her most important works.

Outside of academia, *A Room of One's Own* continues to make an impact. Among those influenced is the Nobel Prize-winning South African novelist J. M. Coetzee,* whose 2003 novel *Elizabeth Costello* takes its central inspiration from *A Room*'s innovative hybrid form, following a female novelist as she delivers a series of fictionalized lectures in various contexts.

> *"Of course criticism has taken many a narrative turn before, though it was obviously Virginia Woolf's **A Room of One's Own** and (to a lesser extent) her **Three Guineas** that inspired my efforts."*
>
> Susan Gubar, *Rooms of Our Own*

Interaction

Susan Gubar's *Rooms of Our Own* shows the strong influence of both Woolf and the essay among feminist literary critics. Gubar identifies Woolf as central to her work, and in *Rooms of Our Own* she explores that influence with the same hybrid mixture of fiction and critical writing that Woolf uses in her essay. The book traces a year in the life of an English professor at an American university, taking direct inspiration from *A Room of One's Own*, with Gubar christening her narrator Mary Beton, as Woolf does hers.

Rooms of Our Own is a meditation on both female experience in the present day and on issues that have become central to feminism since Woolf's time: "the disentangling of gender from sex, of social roles from biological genitalia, of masculinity from males and femininity from females."[2] Placing this list in the distinctively Woolfean mouth of her own narrator, Gubar shows just how much feminism has changed since Woolf's time, and how relevant Woolf's approach might still be.

J. M. Coetzee is less explicit about his debt to Woolf. *Elizabeth Costello* takes as its main character an aging Australian novelist and follows her as she gives lectures on a range of topics, including animal rights. Early in the novel, the reader learns that Woolf is an influential figure in Costello's life and, like Woolf, she is pressured to give her thoughts on a range of "big questions," including "the woman question."[3] Woolf's influence is even more obvious in the actual creation of the novel: it does not just portray lectures, but actually consists of them. "Elizabeth Costello" was a persona adopted by Coetzee to deliver lectures in real life, just as Woolf adopted "Mary Beton."

The Continuing Debate

As Elaine Showalter's criticism suggests, *A Room of One's Own* is as controversial for its methodology as for its findings. Toril Moi notes that Showalter and others want *A Room* to give "a firm perspective from which to judge the world." But the essay remains hard to pin down behind its narrator, its humor, and its irony.[4] That method remains controversial, running counter to the accepted conventions of political and academic writing.

Similar critiques were aimed at Coetzee's *Elizabeth Costello*, which started life as pieces written for the Tanner Lectures (on philosophy and ethics) at Princeton University in 1997–98. Rather than give conventional lectures, Coetzee read two stories about a female novelist giving lectures. Originally published with responses from four philosophers as *The Lives of the Animals* (1999), the pieces caused controversy. As the novelist and critic David Lodge* noted in his review of *Elizabeth Costello*, the respondents felt "stymied" by the "veils of fiction behind which [Coetzee] had concealed his own position."[5] As James Wood put it, Coetzee was accused by the philosopher Peter Singer* of "evasion."[6] Like Woolf, whose influence is clear in *Elizabeth Costello*'s central device, critics wanted Coetzee to speak without resorting to fiction.

Susan Gubar anticipated similar critiques of her use of "narrative criticism" in *Rooms of Our Own*. Readers might say that no "new advance in knowledge can be made without ... footnotes and judicious specificity ... careful reasoning and historical archiving."[7] She suggests, though, that Woolf's method remains useful, and necessary "when multiple perspectives, contradictory convictions, more concrete approaches to interconnected cultural problems have to be broached."[8] As she says, Woolf's investigative techniques remain contentious, but might be vital in grappling with the issues that continue to confront us today.

1 See Susan Gubar, *Rooms of Our Own* (Champaign: University of Illinois Press, 2006).

2 Gubar, *Rooms of Our Own*, 2.

3 J. M. Coetzee, *Elizabeth Costello* (London: Vintage, 2004), 10.

4 Toril Moi, *Textual/Sexual Politics*, 2nd edn (London: Routledge, 2002), 9.

5 David Lodge, "Disturbing the Peace: *Elizabeth Costello* by J. M. Coetzee," *New York Review of Books,* November 20, 2003, accessed September 21, 2015, http://www.nybooks.com/articles/archives/2003/nov/20/disturbing-the-peace/.

6 James Wood, "A Frog's Life: *Elizabeth Costello: Eight Lessons* by J. M. Coetzee," *London Review of Books* 25, no. 20 (October 23, 2003), 15.

7 Gubar, *Rooms of Our Own*, 217.

8 Gubar, *Rooms of Our Own*, 218.

MODULE 12
WHERE NEXT?

KEY POINTS

- Given Virginia Woolf's place in the literary canon,* and the continuing relevance of its issues today, *A Room of One's Own* looks set to remain an important text.

- In the future the essay will continue to engage new readers and influence critics, writers, and feminist* thinkers today.

- *A Room* remains a seminal text, and a crucial document in the history of feminism and literary theory.

Potential

It seems indisputable that Virginia Woolf's *A Room of One's Own* will continue to have a place in literary studies and feminism. Despite the huge advances in women's rights and social freedoms since 1928, Woolf's analysis of the ways in which social convention and economic conditions force women into certain roles and constrain them physically, psychologically, and creatively remains powerful and influential. As the work of the literary critic Susan Gubar* and the novelist J. M. Coetzee* shows, the essay's influence continues to be felt today, providing ways of examining feminist issues and other ethical problems that are still unconventional.

One factor ensuring the place of *A Room of One's Own* in the canon of key texts in feminist history is Woolf's influence as a novelist. Woolf is a fixture of literature syllabuses across the English-speaking world. She is regarded as a groundbreaking innovator in fiction and a crucial figure in the history of literature. *A Room* is the most direct of Woolf's texts to address the conditions of writing as a woman in the early twentieth century. It is a vital document in understanding her development. More broadly, however, it remains a powerful text for understanding and analyzing the ways in which the everyday, material conditions of life affect writers' minds—whether or not they are the female writers Woolf intended to examine.

Though necessarily limited in its own historical perspective, and bound up with certain standard assumptions of an age and place in which class and racial oppression were the norm, *A Room of One's Own* appears likely to continue providing inspiration in a number of fields. Feminism has developed in ways that Woolf could never have imagined. It is an ever more theoretically complex field, linked to gender studies, queer theory,* and postcolonial theory* (the theoretical inquiry into the various legacies of colonialism). But Woolf's essay remains a touchstone.

> *"[The] opportunity will come, and the dead poet who was Shakespeare's sister will put on the body which she has so often laid down. Drawing her life from the lives of the unknown who were her forerunners, as her brother did before her, she will be born."*
>
> ——Virginia Woolf, *A Room of One's Own*

Future Directions

It is hard to predict the directions critics of *A Room of One's Own* will take in the future. Clearly, though, as consideration of the limits of Woolf's "room" continues, and efforts to resurrect writers obscured by circumstance or hegemony (political or cultural domination) persist, this text will contribute to future intellectual work. *A Room* is enduringly valuable for its insistence that women's lives should not be confined to domestic realms, and that creative or professional pursuits, as well as independent lifestyles, are both possible and acceptable.

It is true that in many countries today, the disparities between women's and men's opportunities and economic conditions have shrunk. Nowadays, British women are able to pursue education, careers, and creative endeavors without facing the barriers met by Woolf and her first readers. However, disparity persists between men and women and between other dominant and minority social groups in these realms. Cultural expectations of women's domestic obligations and inclinations also remain in flux. From a global perspective, women's educational, professional, and artistic opportunities are still far more narrowly constrained than those of men. While *A Room of One's Own* maintains its relevance it is sure to encourage current and future debate on these topics.

As the American novelist Alice Walker's* application of Woolf's framework to the experience of black women in American history shows, Woolf's ideas are not restricted to her original audience.[1] By making a link between material conditions and creative efforts, *A Room of One's Own* offers a valuable example for debate over the means necessary for artistic production. It can also be used to argue for the rights of all citizens to earn those means—whether they be women or members of any other group disadvantaged by prevailing social conditions.

Summary

Today, anyone with an interest in the development of the novel, in women's writing, or in feminism should read *A Room of One's Own* as a text that is both historically important and of continuing relevance. The essay deserves special attention because of its unique blend of literary and critical modes, its powerful and practical argument for women's rights, its place in Virginia Woolf's wider work, and its lasting textual strength. Woolf's works enjoy a prominent place in the literary canon today, studied by scholars around the world. Her work in modernist* fiction as well as her critical engagements with literary genres, modern aesthetics, and social issues have made her a unique presence in Anglophone literature. *A Room* is evidence of that status and of the kinds of challenges Woolf faced in achieving her goals.

The essay has a specific historical context, and there are limitations to Woolf's perspective. But these very limitations have prompted further critical engagement, underscoring the text's foundational importance. Critics such as Alice Walker have pointed out that the essay's central argument cannot speak for all women or all would-be writers across history. But they have also worked to expand Woolf's room so that it might be available to more identities and other voices. That this was Woolf's hope for her text's legacy can hardly be questioned.

In discussing the seminal status and sophistication of *A Room of One's Own* we must not forget its readability. It is not just an important essay: it is also an engaging, involving, and persuasive text that stands on its own, as well as forming a perfect introduction to Woolf's work and to feminist literary theory.

1 See Alice Walker, *In Search of Our Mothers' Gardens: Womanist Prose* (London: Phoenix, 2005).

 **GLOSSARY OF TERMS**

1. **Antifeminism:** an umbrella term for ideological opposition to feminism.

2. **Androgyny:** a term for a combination of masculine and feminine characteristics, whether biological or psychological.

3. **Bloomsbury Group:** an influential set of English writers, artists, philosophers, and intellectuals—including Virginia Woolf, John Maynard Keynes, and E. M. Forster—who formed a loose collective in and around Bloomsbury Square in London.

4. **Bohemian:** a term for socially unconventional people, particularly writers, intellectuals, artists, and actors, often espousing antiestablishment or politically radical views.

5. **Cultural materialism:** a critical movement that analyzes works of art through the material conditions of their production. Though often credited to the postwar British literary critic Raymond Williams, its roots can be traced back to the work of the German economist and political philosopher Karl Marx (1818–83).

6. **Elizabethan era:** a period of English history and culture covered by the reign of Queen Elizabeth I in the years 1558–1603.

7. **Feminism:** a set of movements and ideologies seeking to achieve equality for women.

8. **First-wave feminism:** a late nineteenth- and early twentieth-century women's movement, active principally in Britain and North America, which sought equal legal standing with men, particularly the right to vote.

9. **Girton College:** one of the constituent colleges of the University of Cambridge; established in 1869, it was a female-only college until 1976 when they voted to admit men.

10. **Hogarth Press:** a publishing imprint started in 1917 by Virginia and Leonard Woolf at their home, Hogarth House, in Richmond. Together with Woolf's own writing, it is notable for publishing the first book edition of T. S. Eliot's *The Waste Land*.

11 **Literary canon:** a term for the set of literary works across history that have

traditionally been accepted as the most influential and worthy of study by scholars and academics.

12. **Misogyny:** the hatred of women.

13. **Modernism:** a broad movement in the arts characterized both by a break with traditional formal constraints and a heavy investment in artistic traditions and lineage. In literature, landmark figures were Virginia Woolf, T. S. Eliot, and James Joyce, all of whom produced groundbreaking works in the first third of the twentieth century.

14. **Newnham College:** one of the constituent colleges of the University of Cambridge; founded as a women's college in 1871, it remains female-only to this day.

15. **Patriarchy:** a term for a social system in which men hold the primary power, social privileges, and authority. In feminist theory, Western society is seen as pervasively patriarchal.

16. **Postcolonial theory:** a broad category of critical and philosophical work dealing with the cultural and intellectual legacies of colonialism and imperialism in former colonies of Western nations, including Britain, France, and Spain.

17. **Postwar period:** the period immediately following World War II in Europe and America.

18. **Psychoanalysis:** a set of theories for treating psychological illness, first elaborated by Austrian physician Sigmund Freud at the end of the nineteenth century.

19. **Queer theory:** a broad field of theory associated with literary studies, women's studies, and cultural studies that is concerned with inquiry into supposedly deviant sexual identities.

20. **Second-wave feminism:** feminism of the postwar era often strongly influenced by French feminist theory and focused on issues such as women's sexual freedom, workplace equality, and reproductive rights.

21. **Stream of consciousness:** a term for a narrative technique that mimics the

thinking processes of a character, directly portraying their perceptions of narrative events through their thoughts.

22. **Suffrage:** the right to vote in public elections; often refers specifically to the women's suffrage movement of first-wave feminism.

23. **Suffragette:** a term for female members of the women's movement's campaign for women's voting rights (suffrage) in the nineteenth and early twentieth centuries; it was particularly reserved for more militant campaigners.

24. **Textual:** literally, like or relating to a text; often used metaphorically to describe society in philosophy, sociology, and literary theory to suggest that social structures can be "read" like a book or text.

25. **University of Cambridge:** the second university founded in England, in 1209; composed of 31 colleges, it is widely regarded as one of the world's most prestigious universities.

26. **Women's movement:** an umbrella term for the women's liberation or feminist movement. It is also often applied specifically to early feminism and the movement for women's suffrage.

27. **World War I:** a global conflict from 1914 to 1918 that centered on clashes in Europe between Germany–Austria–Hungary, the "Central Powers," and the Allies—Britain, France, and Russia.

28. **World War II:** the global war of 1939–45 involving over 30 countries in a conflict over the expansionist policies of Nazi Germany and its allies.

PEOPLE MENTIONED IN THE TEXT

1. **Jane Austen (1775–1817)** was an English novelist renowned for her closely observed satirical fiction based on the society of her day. These works are among the most celebrated in the English literary canon, and include *Pride and Prejudice* (1813) and *Emma* (1815).

2. **Aphra Behn (circa 1640–89)** was an English playwright and poet. The first major female writer in English drama, she was among the earliest professional female writers; her best-known works today are the play *The Rover* (in two parts, 1677 and 1681) and the prose fiction *Oroonoko* (1688).

3. **Clive Bell (1881–1964)** was an English art critic and author who advocated the significance of form over subject matter in art. A member of the Bloomsbury Group, he was married to Virginia Woolf's sister, Vanessa.

4. **Vanessa Bell (née Stephen; 1879–1961)** was an English painter, illustrator, and designer; Virginia Woolf's sister, she was a member of the Bloomsbury Group and wife of Clive Bell.

5. **Arnold Bennett (1867–1931)** was an English novelist, journalist, and critic. A prolific writer, he remains perhaps best known for his 1908 novel *The Old Wives' Tale*.

6. **Rachel Bowlby** is a professor of English literature at Princeton University; she is best known for her influential 1988 study *Virginia Woolf: Feminist Destinations*.

7. **Brontë sisters** were influential English female novelists of the early nineteenth century. **Charlotte (1816–55)**, the most prolific, is best remembered for *Jane Eyre* (1847); **Emily (1818–48)** wrote only one novel, *Wuthering Heights* (1847); **Anne (1820–49)** wrote two, *Agnes Grey* (1847) and *The Tenant of Wildfell Hall* (1848).

8. **Hélène Cixous (b. 1937)** is an influential French feminist writer and philosopher, considered one of the mothers of poststructuralist feminist theory. She is widely known for her 1975 article "The Laugh of the Medusa," and her elaboration of the idea of *écriture féminine* ("feminine writing").

9. **Edward Clarke (1820–77)** was a medical doctor and professor of medicine

at Harvard University. He is remembered today for his misguided stance on women's education in his *Sex in Education; or, A Fair Chance for Girls* (1873).

10. **J. M. Coetzee (b. 1940)** is a Nobel Prize-winning South African novelist, essayist, and translator.The author of 12 novels and 4 volumes of fictionalized autobiography, he is widely considered to be one of the world's most important living novelists.

11. **Fyodor Dostoevsky (1821–81)** was a Russian novelist, regarded as one of the most important writers of the nineteenth century; his most famous works are *Crime and Punishment* (1866) and *The Brothers Karamazov* (1880).

12. **George Eliot (1819–80)** was the pen name of the novelist Mary Ann Evans. Widely considered one of the most important writers in the history of the novel, her best-known works include *The Mill on the Floss* (1860) and *Middlemarch* (1872).

13. **T. S. Eliot (1888–1965)** was an American-born poet and critic who was at the forefront of British modernism. His most famous works include the long poems *The Waste Land* (1922) and *Four Quartets* (1945), and the seminal critical essay "Tradition and the Individual Talent" (1919).

14. **E. M. Forster (1879–1970)** was an English novelist, essayist, literary critic, and Bloomsbury Group member. His fiction includes *A Passage to India* (1908), *Howard's End* (1910), and the homosexually themed *Maurice* (1971), which was written in 1913–14 but not published until after his death.

15. **Roger Fry (1866–1934)** was an English painter and art critic. A member of the Bloomsbury Group, he is known for christening the genre of postimpressionist painting.

16. **Margaret Fuller (1810–50)** was an American journalist and early feminist; her book *Woman in the Nineteenth Century* (1843) is considered perhaps the first American feminist work.

17. **Charlotte Perkins Gilman (1860–1935)** was a prominent American feminist and writer; her book *Women and Economics: A Study of the Economic*

Relation Between Men and Women as a Factor in Social Evolution (1898) is a seminal text in the history of feminism.

18. **Susan Gubar (b. 1944)** is an American author, feminist literary critic, and professor of English and women's studies at Indiana University. She is best known today for coauthoring (with Sandra M. Gilbert) *The Madwoman in the Attic:The Woman Writer and the Nineteenth-Century Literary Imagination* (1979).

19. **Cicely Hamilton (1872–1952)** was an English actress, writer, and feminist; she was the co-founder of the Women Writers' Suffrage League in 1908.

20. **James Joyce (1882–1941)** was an Irish novelist and pioneering member of the modernist movement. He is best known for his novels *Ulysses* (1922) and *Finnegan's Wake* (1939).

21. **John Maynard Keynes (1883–1946)** was an influential English economist whose work in macroeconomics revolutionized the discipline.

22. **D. H. Lawrence (1885–1930)** was an English novelist, poet, and critic whose controversial novel *Lady Chatterley's Lover* (1928) is considered a landmark in the development of the novel.

23. **David Lodge (b. 1935)** is an English novelist and critic known for his satirical novels about academic life and for his literary criticism, particularly the essays collected in *The Art of Fiction* (1992).

24. **Toril Moi (b. 1953)** is a Norwegian-born feminist theorist and literary critic. Currently James B. Duke professor of literature and romance studies and professor of English, philosophy, and theatre studies at Duke University, she is best known for *Sexual/Textual Politics: Feminist Literary Theory* (1985) and *What is a Woman? And Other Essays* (1999).

25. **Ezra Pound (1885–1972)** was an American poet whose work helped found the modernist movement; he is best known for his complex, allusive epic poem sequence *The Cantos* (1917–69).

26. **Arthur Quiller-Couch (1863–1944)** was an English writer and literary critic.

Though prolific in several genres, he is now best remembered for editing *The Oxford Book of English Verse 1250–1900* (1900).

27. **Eleanor Rathbone (1872–1946)** was an English feminist and independent Member of Parliament. She was a prominent and long-term campaigner for women's rights in Britain.

28. **Elizabeth Robins (1862–1952)** was an American actress, playwright, and suffragette. After moving to England in 1888, she became involved in the women's movement, writing the influential suffrage play *Votes for Women!* (1907).

29. **Vita Sackville-West (1892–1962)** was a poet, novelist, and journalist, also known as an important garden designer. Famous for having a number of extramarital affairs with women, she had a relationship with Virginia Woolf, and inspired Woolf's novel *Orlando: A Biography*.

30. **Sappho (circa 630–570 B.C.E.)** was a noted Greek lyric poet, born on the island of Lesbos. Though only fragments of her work survive today, she is famous for her love poetry addressed to both women and men; indeed, her name was almost synonymous with lesbianism until the mid-twentieth century.

31. **Olive Schreiner (1855–1920)** was a South African author, antiwar campaigner, and early feminist. Today she is best known for her novel *The Story of an African Farm* (1883) and the feminist work *Women and Labour* (1911).

32. **William Shakespeare (1564–1616)** was an English poet and playwright, the author of 154 sonnets and 38 plays, many of which are core works in the study of English literature, as well as living texts, constantly kept alive in performance throughout the world. He is known as England's national poet.

33. **Elaine Showalter (b. 1941)** is an American feminist literary critic known for developing "gynocriticsm"; her best-known works are *Towards a Feminist Poetics* (1979) and *Inventing Herself: Claiming a Feminist Literary Heritage* (2001).

34. **Peter Singer (b. 1946)** is an Australian moral philosopher and professor of bioethics at Princeton University; he is best known for his 1975 work *Animal Liberation*, regarded as a classic work on animal rights.

35. **Adrian Stephen (1883–1948)** was the younger brother of Virginia Woolf and a member of the Bloomsbury Group. A pioneering adopter of Sigmund Freud's theories, he was among the first British psychoanalysts.

36. **Leslie Stephen (1832–1904)** was an English author, critic, and biographer. The father of Virginia Woolf, he is best known today as the founding editor of the *Dictionary of National Biography*.

37. **Thoby Stephen (1880–1906)** was the older brother of Virginia Woolf; he is often credited with starting the Bloomsbury Group's gatherings.

38. **Lytton Strachey (1880–1932)** was an English biographer and member of the Bloomsbury Group.Today he is best known for his 1918 biographical work *Eminent Victorians*.

39. **Ray Strachey (née Costelloe; 1887–1940)** was an English feminist politician and writer.Wife of Lytton Strachey's elder brother, Oliver, she is best known today for her role in the suffrage movement and her 1928 book *The Cause: A Short History of the Women's Movement in Great Britain*.

40. **Alice Walker (b. 1944)** is an American author, feminist, and activist known for her 1982 novel *The Color Purple* and her 1983 essay collection *In Search of Our Mothers' Gardens:Womanist Prose*.

41. **Otto Weininger (1880–1903)** was an Austrian philosopher whose misogynist work *Sex and Character* (1903) rose to international prominence after his suicide.

42. **Phillis Wheatley (1753–84)** was an African American poet and the first African American woman to be published. Sold into slavery in America as a child, her *Poems on Various Subjects, Religious and Moral* (1773) brought her fame and eventually freedom.

43. **Mary Wollstonecraft (1759–97)** was an English writer and philosopher, best

known for her groundbreaking feminist tract *A Vindication of the Rights of Woman* (1792).

44. **Leonard Woolf (1880–1969)** was Virginia Woolf's husband from 1912 until her death in 1941. A member of the Bloomsbury Group, he was a noted publisher and author, co-founding the Hogarth Press with his wife and composing a number of works on political theory.

 **WORKS CITED**

1. Antor, Heinz. *The Bloomsbury Group: Its Philosophy, Aesthetics, and Literary Achievement*. Heidelberg: C. Winter, 1986.

2. Barrett, Eileen, and Patricia Cramer, eds. *Virginia Woolf: Lesbian Readings*. New York: New York University Press, 1997.

3. Bennett, Arnold. "Queen of the High-Brows" (review of *A Room of One's Own*, *Evening Standard*, November 28, 1929). In *Virginia Woolf: The Critical Heritage*, edited by Robin Majumdar and Allen McLaurin. London: Routledge & Kegan Paul, 1975.

4. Bowlby, Rachel. *Feminist Destinations and Further Essays on Virginia Woolf*. Oxford: Blackwell, 1997.

5. Briggs, Julia. *Virginia Woolf: An Inner Life*. Orlando: Harcourt, 2005.

6. Cixous, Hélène. "The Laugh of the Medusa." Translated by Keith and Paula Cohen. *Signs* 1, no. 4 (1976): 875–93.

7. Clarke, Edward H. *Sex in Education; or, A Fair Chance for Girls* (1873). In Nancy F. Cott, *Root of Bitterness: Documents of the Social History of American Women*. Lebanon, NH: University Press of New England, 1996.

8. Coetzee, J. M. *Elizabeth Costello*. London: Vintage, 2004.

9. Eliot, T. S. "Tradition and the Individual Talent." In *Selected Essays*. London: Faber & Faber, 1951.

10. Fuller, Margaret. *Woman in the Nineteenth Century*. Edited by Arthur B. Fuller. New York: W. W. Norton, 1971.

11. Gilman, Charlotte Perkins. *The Man-Made World: Or, Our Androcentric Culture*. New York: Charlton, 1911.

12. Goldman, Jane. *The Cambridge Introduction to Virginia Woolf*. Cambridge: Cambridge University Press, 2006.

13. Gubar, Susan. "Introduction." In Virginia Woolf, *A Room of One's Own*, edited by Susan Gubar. Orlando: Harcourt, 2005.

14. ———. *Rooms of Our Own*. Champaign: University of Illinois Press, 2006.

15. Hamilton, Cicely. *Marriage as a Trade*. New York: Moffat, Yard and Co., 1909.

16. Keegan, John. *The First World War*. New York: Vintage, 2000.

17. Lee, Hermione. *Virginia Woolf*. London: Vintage, 1997.

18. Lodge, David. "Disturbing the Peace: *Elizabeth Costello* by J. M. Coetzee." *New*

York Review of Books, November 20, 2003. Accessed September 21, 2015. http://www.nybooks.com/articles/archives/2003/nov/20/disturbing-the-peace/

19. Maddison, Angus. *The World Economy: A Millennial Perspective*. Paris: Organisation for Economic Co-Operation and Development, 2001.

20. Majumdar, Robin, and Allen McLaurin, eds. *Virginia Woolf: The Critical Heritage*. London: Routledge & Kegan Paul, 1975.

21. Marcus, Jane. *Art and Anger: Reading Like a Woman*. Columbus: Ohio State University Press, 1988.

22. ———. *Virginia Woolf and the Languages of Patriarchy*. Bloomington: Indiana University Press, 1987.

23. Marcus, Laura. *Virginia Woolf*. 2nd edn. Tavistock: Northcote House, 2004.

24. McWilliams-Tullberg, Rita. *Women at Cambridge: A Men's University, Though of a Mixed Type*. London: Gollancz, 1975.

25. Minow-Pinkney, Makiko. *Virginia Woolf and the Problem of the Subject*. Edinburgh: Edinburgh University Press, 2010.

26. Moi, Toril. *Sexual/Textual Politics: Feminist Literary Theory*. 2nd edn. London: Routledge, 2002.

27. Park, Sowon S. "Suffrage and Virginia Woolf: 'The Mass Behind the Single Voice'." *The Review of English Studies* 56, no. 223 (2005): 119–34.

28. Quiller-Couch, Arthur. *On the Art of Writing*. New York: G. P. Putnam's Sons, 1916.

29. Robbins, Rae Gallant. *The Bloomsbury Group: A Selective Bibliography*. 1st edn. Kenmore, WA: Price Guide Publishers, 1978.

30. Sarkar, Tapan K., Robert J. Mailloux, Arthur A. Oliner, Magdalena Salazar-Palma, and Dipak L. Sengupta. *History of Wireless*. Hoboken, NJ: Wiley-Interscience, 2006.

31. Schreiner, Olive. *Woman and Labour*. London: T. Fisher Unwin, 1911.

32. Showalter, Elaine. *A Literature of Their Own: From Charlotte Brontë to Doris Lessing*. Princeton: Princeton University Press, 1999.

33. Spalding, Frances. *The Bloomsbury Group*. London: National Portrait Gallery, 2005.

34. Walker, Alice. *In Search of Our Mothers' Gardens: Womanist Prose*. London:

Phoenix, 2005.

35. Weininger, Otto. *Sex and Character* (London: William Heinemann, 1906).

36. Whitworth, Michael H. *Virginia Woolf.* Oxford: Oxford University Press, 2005.

37. Wollstonecraft, Mary. *A Vindication of the Rights of Woman.* Edited by Deidre Shauna Lynch. New York: W. W. Norton, 2009.

38. Wood, James. "A Frog's Life: *Elizabeth Costello: Eight Lessons* by J. M. Coetzee." *London Review of Books* 25, no. 20 (October 23, 2003): 15–16.

39. Woolf, Virginia. *A Room of One's Own* and *Three Guineas.* Edited by Anna Snaith. Oxford: Oxford University Press, 2015.

40. ———. *Women & Fiction: The Manuscript Versions of A Room of One's Own.* Edited by S. P. Rosenbaum. Oxford: Blackwell, 1992.

41. ———.*Women and Writing.* Edited by Michèle Barrett. London: Women's Press, 1979.

42. ———. *A Writer's Diary.* Edited by Leonard Woolf. London: Harcourt, 1954.

43. Zwerdling, Alex. *Virginia Woolf and the Real World.* Berkeley: University of California Press, 1986.

原书作者简介

弗吉尼亚·伍尔芙是 20 世纪二三十年代布卢姆斯伯里激进知识分子文化团体中的一员干将，同时是当时伦敦著名的作家、艺术家和改革家。1882 年，她出身于一个上层知识分子家庭，在家里接受教育。1915 年出版第一部小说，1941 年去世，一生共写了 8 部小说。

《达洛维夫人》和《到灯塔去》两本书奠定了伍尔芙 20 世纪最伟大小说家的地位。尽管她出身于英国上层社会，却经历并且体会到女性日常生活中遭遇到的种种压迫。她的女权主义理论思考，激发了她 1929 年写下《一间自己的房间》。该文本在女性写作中具有开创性价值，至今在许多探讨社会不公正领域中仍具有参考价值。

本书作者简介

菲奥娜·鲁滨逊博士于 21 世纪初在耶鲁大学获得英语文学博士学位。

蒂姆·史密斯-莱恩博士在牛津大学默顿学院获得哲学博士学位，在牛津大学耶稣学院和巴黎政治学院任职。

世界名著中的批判性思维

《世界思想宝库钥匙丛书》致力于深入浅出地阐释全世界著名思想家的观点，不论是谁、在何处都能了解到，从而推进批判性思维发展。

《世界思想宝库钥匙丛书》与世界顶尖大学的一流学者合作，为一系列学科中最有影响的著作推出新的分析文本，介绍其观点和影响。在这一不断扩展的系列中，每种选入的著作都代表了历经时间考验的思想典范。通过为这些著作提供必要背景、揭示原作者的学术渊源以及说明这些著作所产生的影响，本系列图书希望让读者以新视角看待这些划时代的经典之作。读者应学会思考、运用并挑战这些著作中的观点，而不是简单接受它们。

ABOUT THE AUTHOR OF THE ORIGINAL WORK

Virginia Woolf was one of the Bloomsbury Group of radical intellectuals, writers, artists, and innovators, who were famous in London in the 1920s and 1930s. Born in 1882 into an upper-class intellectual family, she was educated at home and published her first novel in 1915, writing eight in total before her death in 1941.

Works such as *Mrs Dalloway* and *To The Lighthouse* ensured Woolf's reputation as one of the greatest novelists of the twentieth century. Although she came from a privileged background, she nevertheless experienced and understood the everyday oppression of women. Her theories on feminism inspired her 1929 essay *A Room of One's Own*. It remains a seminal text in feminist writing, and is still relevant today in many areas of social injustice.

ABOUT THE AUTHORS OF THE ANALYSIS

Dr Fiona Robinson holds a PhD in early twenty-first century English literature from Yale University.

Dr Tim Smith-Laing took his DPhil at Merton College, Oxford, and has held positions at Jesus College, Oxford, and Sciences Po in Paris.

ABOUT MACAT
GREAT WORKS FOR CRITICAL THINKING

Macat is focused on making the ideas of the world's great thinkers accessible and comprehensible to everybody, everywhere, in ways that promote the development of enhanced critical thinking skills.

It works with leading academics from the world's top universities to produce new analyses that focus on the ideas and the impact of the most influential works ever written across a wide variety of academic disciplines. Each of the works that sit at the heart of its growing library is an enduring example of great thinking. But by setting them in context—and looking at the influences that shaped their authors, as well as the responses they provoked—Macat encourages readers to look at these classics and game-changers with fresh eyes. Readers learn to think, engage and challenge their ideas, rather than simply accepting them.

批判性思维与《一间自己的房间》

首要批判性思维技巧：创造性思维

次要批判性思维技巧：理性化思维

《一间自己的房间》非常清晰地展现了创造性的思想家们如何从新颖的角度联系和表达事物。

《房间》成书于弗吉尼亚·伍尔芙在剑桥女子学院的一次演讲，主题是"女性与小说"。伍尔芙的切入点是质询为何在 20 世纪初的文学史里鲜有伟大的女性作家。当时的社会偏见将此归于（也用于辅证）女性较于男性创造力低下。伍尔芙抗议道，恰恰相反，这种现象缘于一个简单的事实：自古以来，男性统治的社会系统性地阻碍着女人们拥有教育的机会、私人的空间和创造艺术需要的经济独立。在一个普遍认为"艺术"仅限于思想范畴、与经济条件毫无干系的时代，这是一个新奇的提议。更新奇的是伍尔芙争论和证明观点的方式：通过虚构作品展现一个极富特权的女人在日常生活中仍频频受限。作为一个令人印象深刻的早期文化唯物主义的范例，《一间自己的房间》对创造性思维的提炼与浓缩极具代表性。

CRITICAL THINKING AND *A ROOM OF ONE'S OWN*

• Primary critical thinking skill: CREATIVE THINKING
• Secondary critical thinking skill: REASONING

A Room of One's Own is a very clear example of how creative thinkers connect and present things in novel ways.

Based on the text of a talk given by Virginia Woolf at an all-female Cambridge college, *Room* considers the subject of "women and fiction." Woolf's approach is to ask why, in the early 20th century, literary history presented so few examples of canonically "great" women writers. The common prejudices of the time suggested this was caused by (and proof of) women's creative and intellectual inferiority to men. Woolf argued instead that it was to do with a very simple fact: across the centuries, male-dominated society had systematically prevented women from having the educational opportunities, private spaces and economic independence to produce great art. At a time when "art" was commonly considered to be a province of the mind that had no relation to economic circumstances, this was a novel proposal. More novel, though, was Woolf's manner of arguing and proving her contentions: through a fictional account of the limits placed on even the most privileged women in everyday existence. An impressive early example of cultural materialism, *A Room of One's Own* is an exemplary encapsulation of creative thinking.

《世界思想宝库钥匙丛书》简介

《世界思想宝库钥匙丛书》致力于为一系列在各领域产生重大影响的人文社科类经典著作提供独特的学术探讨。每一本读物都不仅仅是原经典著作的内容摘要，而是介绍并深入研究原经典著作的学术渊源、主要观点和历史影响。这一丛书的目的是提供一套学习资料，以促进读者掌握批判性思维，从而更全面、深刻地去理解重要思想。

每一本读物分为 3 个部分：学术渊源、学术思想和学术影响，每个部分下有 4 个小节。这些章节旨在从各个方面研究原经典著作及其反响。

由于独特的体例，每一本读物不但易于阅读，而且另有一项优点：所有读物的编排体例相同，读者在进行某个知识层面的调查或研究时可交叉参阅多本该丛书中的相关读物，从而开启跨领域研究的路径。

为了方便阅读，每本读物最后还列出了术语表和人名表（在书中则以星号＊标记），此外还有参考文献。

《世界思想宝库钥匙丛书》与剑桥大学合作，理清了批判性思维的要点，即如何通过 6 种技能来进行有效思考。其中 3 种技能让我们能够理解问题，另 3 种技能让我们有能力解决问题。这 6 种技能合称为"批判性思维 PACIER 模式"，它们是：

分析：了解如何建立一个观点；
评估：研究一个观点的优点和缺点；
阐释：对意义所产生的问题加以理解；
创造性思维：提出新的见解，发现新的联系；
解决问题：提出切实有效的解决办法；
理性化思维：创建有说服力的观点。

了解更多信息，请浏览 www.macat.com。

THE MACAT LIBRARY

The Macat Library is a series of unique academic explorations of seminal works in the humanities and social sciences — books and papers that have had a significant and widely recognised impact on their disciplines. It has been created to serve as much more than just a summary of what lies between the covers of a great book. It illuminates and explores the influences on, ideas of, and impact of that book. Our goal is to offer a learning resource that encourages critical thinking and fosters a better, deeper understanding of important ideas.

Each publication is divided into three Sections: Influences, Ideas, and Impact. Each Section has four Modules. These explore every important facet of the work, and the responses to it.

This Section-Module structure makes a Macat Library book easy to use, but it has another important feature. Because each Macat book is written to the same format, it is possible (and encouraged!) to cross-reference multiple Macat books along the same lines of inquiry or research. This allows the reader to open up interesting interdisciplinary pathways.

To further aid your reading, lists of glossary terms and people mentioned are included at the end of this book (these are indicated by an asterisk [*] throughout) — as well as a list of works cited.

Macat has worked with the University of Cambridge to identify the elements of critical thinking and understand the ways in which six different skills combine to enable effective thinking.

Three allow us to fully understand a problem; three more give us the tools to solve it. Together, these six skills make up the PACIER model of critical thinking. They are:

ANALYSIS — understanding how an argument is built
EVALUATION — exploring the strengths and weaknesses of an argument
INTERPRETATION — understanding issues of meaning
CREATIVE THINKING — coming up with new ideas and fresh connections
PROBLEM-SOLVING — producing strong solutions
REASONING — creating strong arguments

To find out more, visit WWW.MACAT.COM.

"《世界思想宝库钥匙丛书》提供了独一无二的跨学科学习和研究工具。它介绍那些革新了各自学科研究的经典著作，还邀请全世界一流专家和教育机构进行严谨的分析，为每位读者打开世界顶级教育的大门。"

—— 安德烈亚斯·施莱歇尔，
经济合作与发展组织教育与技能司司长

"《世界思想宝库钥匙丛书》直面大学教育的巨大挑战……他们组建了一支精干而活跃的学者队伍，来推出在研究广度上颇具新意的教学材料。"

—— 布罗尔斯教授、勋爵，剑桥大学前校长

"《世界思想宝库钥匙丛书》的愿景令人赞叹。它通过分析和阐释那些曾深刻影响人类思想以及社会、经济发展的经典文本，提供了新的学习方法。它推动批判性思维，这对于任何社会和经济体来说都是至关重要的。这就是未来的学习方法。"

—— 查尔斯·克拉克阁下，英国前教育大臣

"对于那些影响了各自领域的著作，《世界思想宝库钥匙丛书》能让人们立即了解到围绕那些著作展开的评论性言论，这让该系列图书成为在这些领域从事研究的师生们不可或缺的资源。"

—— 威廉·特朗佐教授，加利福尼亚大学圣地亚哥分校

"Macat offers an amazing first-of-its-kind tool for interdisciplinary learning and research. Its focus on works that transformed their disciplines and its rigorous approach, drawing on the world's leading experts and educational institutions, opens up a world-class education to anyone."

—— Andreas Schleicher, Director for Education and Skills, Organisation for Economic Co-operation and Development

"Macat is taking on some of the major challenges in university education... They have drawn together a strong team of active academics who are producing teaching materials that are novel in the breadth of their approach."

—— Prof Lord Broers, former Vice-Chancellor of the University of Cambridge

"The Macat vision is exceptionally exciting. It focuses upon new modes of learning which analyse and explain seminal texts which have profoundly influenced world thinking and so social and economic development. It promotes the kind of critical thinking which is essential for any society and economy. This is the learning of the future."

—— Rt Hon Charles Clarke, former UK Secretary of State for Education

"The Macat analyses provide immediate access to the critical conversation surrounding the books that have shaped their respective discipline, which will make them an invaluable resource to all of those, students and teachers, working in the field."

—— Prof William Tronzo, University of California at San Diego

The Macat Library
世界思想宝库钥匙丛书

TITLE	中文书名	类别
An Analysis of Arjun Appadurai's *Modernity at Large: Cultural Dimensions of Globalisation*	解析阿尔君·阿帕杜莱《消失的现代性：全球化的文化维度》	人类学
An Analysis of Claude Lévi-Strauss's *Structural Anthropology*	解析克劳德·列维-斯特劳斯《结构人类学》	人类学
An Analysis of Marcel Mauss's *The Gift*	解析马塞尔·莫斯《礼物》	人类学
An Analysis of Jared M. Diamond's *Guns, Germs, and Steel: The Fate of Human Societies*	解析贾雷德·戴蒙德《枪炮、病菌与钢铁：人类社会的命运》	人类学
An Analysis of Clifford Geertz's *The Interpretation of Cultures*	解析克利福德·格尔茨《文化的解释》	人类学
An Analysis of Philippe Ariès's *Centuries of Childhood: A Social History of Family Life*	解析菲力浦·阿利埃斯《儿童的世纪：旧制度下的儿童和家庭生活》	人类学
An Analysis of W. Chan Kim & Renée Mauborgne's *Blue Ocean Strategy*	解析金伟灿 / 勒妮·莫博涅《蓝海战略》	商业
An Analysis of John P. Kotter's *Leading Change*	解析约翰·P.科特《领导变革》	商业
An Analysis of Michael E. Porter's *Competitive Strategy: Creating and Sustaining Superior Performance*	解析迈克尔·E.波特《竞争战略：分析产业和竞争对手的技术》	商业
An Analysis of Jean Lave & Etienne Wenger's *Situated Learning: Legitimate Peripheral Participation*	解析琼·莱夫 / 艾蒂纳·温格《情境学习：合法的边缘性参与》	商业
An Analysis of Douglas McGregor's *The Human Side of Enterprise*	解析道格拉斯·麦格雷戈《企业的人性面》	商业
An Analysis of Milton Friedman's *Capitalism and Freedom*	解析米尔顿·弗里德曼《资本主义与自由》	商业
An Analysis of Ludwig von Mises's *The Theory of Money and Credit*	解析路德维希·冯·米塞斯《货币和信用理论》	经济学
An Analysis of Adam Smith's *The Wealth of Nations*	解析亚当·斯密《国富论》	经济学
An Analysis of Thomas Piketty's *Capital in the Twenty-First Century*	解析托马斯·皮凯蒂《21世纪资本论》	经济学
An Analysis of Nassim Nicholas Taleb's *The Black Swan: The Impact of the Highly Improbable*	解析纳西姆·尼古拉斯·塔勒布《黑天鹅：如何应对不可预知的未来》	经济学
An Analysis of Ha-Joon Chang's *Kicking Away the Ladder*	解析张夏准《富国陷阱：发达国家为何踢开梯子》	经济学
An Analysis of Thomas Robert Malthus's *An Essay on the Principle of Population*	解析托马斯·马尔萨斯《人口论》	经济学

An Analysis of John Maynard Keynes's *The General Theory of Employment, Interest and Money*	解析约翰·梅纳德·凯恩斯《就业、利息和货币通论》	经济学
An Analysis of Milton Friedman's *The Role of Monetary Policy*	解析米尔顿·弗里德曼《货币政策的作用》	经济学
An Analysis of Burton G. Malkiel's *A Random Walk Down Wall Street*	解析伯顿·G.马尔基尔《漫步华尔街》	经济学
An Analysis of Friedrich A. Hayek's *The Road to Serfdom*	解析弗里德里希·A.哈耶克《通往奴役之路》	经济学
An Analysis of Charles P. Kindleberger's *Manias, Panics, and Crashes: A History of Financial Crises*	解析查尔斯·P.金德尔伯格《疯狂、惊恐和崩溃：金融危机史》	经济学
An Analysis of Amartya Sen's *Development as Freedom*	解析阿马蒂亚·森《以自由看待发展》	经济学
An Analysis of Rachel Carson's *Silent Spring*	解析蕾切尔·卡森《寂静的春天》	地理学
An Analysis of Charles Darwin's *On the Origin of Species: by Means of Natural Selection, or The Preservation of Favoured Races in the Struggle for Life*	解析查尔斯·达尔文《物种起源》	地理学
An Analysis of World Commission on Environment and Development's *The Brundtland Report, Our Common Future*	解析世界环境与发展委员会《布伦特兰报告：我们共同的未来》	地理学
An Analysis of James E. Lovelock's *Gaia: A New Look at Life on Earth*	解析詹姆斯·E.拉伍洛克《盖娅：地球生命的新视野》	地理学
An Analysis of Paul Kennedy's *The Rise and Fall of the Great Powers: Economic Change and Military Conflict from 1500—2000*	解析保罗·肯尼迪《大国的兴衰：1500—2000年的经济变革与军事冲突》	历史
An Analysis of Janet L. Abu-Lughod's *Before European Hegemony: The World System A. D. 1250—1350*	解析珍妮特·L.阿布-卢格霍德《欧洲霸权之前：1250—1350年的世界体系》	历史
An Analysis of Alfred W. Crosby's *The Columbian Exchange: Biological and Cultural Consequences of 1492*	解析艾尔弗雷德·W.克罗斯比《哥伦布大交换：1492年以后的生物影响和文化冲击》	历史
An Analysis of Tony Judt's *Postwar: A History of Europe since 1945*	解析托尼·贾德《战后欧洲史》	历史
An Analysis of Richard J. Evans's *In Defence of History*	解析理查德·J.艾文斯《捍卫历史》	历史
An Analysis of Eric Hobsbawm's *The Age of Revolution: Europe 1789–1848*	解析艾瑞克·霍布斯鲍姆《革命的年代：欧洲1789—1848年》	历史

An Analysis of Roland Barthes's *Mythologies*	解析罗兰·巴特《神话学》	文学与批判理论
An Analysis of Simon de Beauvoir's *The Second Sex*	解析西蒙娜·德·波伏娃《第二性》	文学与批判理论
An Analysis of Edward W. Said's *Orientalism*	解析爱德华·W. 萨义德《东方主义》	文学与批判理论
An Analysis of Virginia Woolf's *A Room of One's Own*	解析弗吉尼亚·伍尔芙《一间自己的房间》	文学与批判理论
An Analysis of Judith Butler's *Gender Trouble*	解析朱迪斯·巴特勒《性别麻烦》	文学与批判理论
An Analysis of Ferdinand de Saussure's *Course in General Linguistics*	解析费尔迪南·德·索绪尔《普通语言学教程》	文学与批判理论
An Analysis of Susan Sontag's *On Photography*	解析苏珊·桑塔格《论摄影》	文学与批判理论
An Analysis of Walter Benjamin's *The Work of Art in the Age of Mechanical Reproduction*	解析瓦尔特·本雅明《机械复制时代的艺术作品》	文学与批判理论
An Analysis of W.E.B. Du Bois's *The Souls of Black Folk*	解析 W.E.B. 杜博伊斯《黑人的灵魂》	文学与批判理论
An Analysis of Plato's *The Republic*	解析柏拉图《理想国》	哲学
An Analysis of Plato's *Symposium*	解析柏拉图《会饮篇》	哲学
An Analysis of Aristotle's *Metaphysics*	解析亚里士多德《形而上学》	哲学
An Analysis of Aristotle's *Nicomachean Ethics*	解析亚里士多德《尼各马可伦理学》	哲学
An Analysis of Immanuel Kant's *Critique of Pure Reason*	解析伊曼努尔·康德《纯粹理性批判》	哲学
An Analysis of Ludwig Wittgenstein's *Philosophical Investigations*	解析路德维希·维特根斯坦《哲学研究》	哲学
An Analysis of G.W.F. Hegel's *Phenomenology of Spirit*	解析 G.W.F. 黑格尔《精神现象学》	哲学
An Analysis of Baruch Spinoza's *Ethics*	解析巴鲁赫·斯宾诺莎《伦理学》	哲学
An Analysis of Hannah Arendt's *The Human Condition*	解析汉娜·阿伦特《人的境况》	哲学
An Analysis of G.E.M. Anscombe's *Modern Moral Philosophy*	解析 G.E.M. 安斯康姆《现代道德哲学》	哲学
An Analysis of David Hume's *An Enquiry Concerning Human Understanding*	解析大卫·休谟《人类理解研究》	哲学

An Analysis of Søren Kierkegaard's *Fear and Trembling*	解析索伦·克尔凯郭尔《恐惧与战栗》	哲学
An Analysis of René Descartes's *Meditations on First Philosophy*	解析勒内·笛卡尔《第一哲学沉思录》	哲学
An Analysis of Friedrich Nietzsche's *On the Genealogy of Morality*	解析弗里德里希·尼采《论道德的谱系》	哲学
An Analysis of Gilbert Ryle's *The Concept of Mind*	解析吉尔伯特·赖尔《心的概念》	哲学
An Analysis of Thomas Kuhn's *The Structure of Scientific Revolutions*	解析托马斯·库恩《科学革命的结构》	哲学
An Analysis of John Stuart Mill's *Utilitarianism*	解析约翰·斯图亚特·穆勒《功利主义》	哲学
An Analysis of Aristotle's *Politics*	解析亚里士多德《政治学》	政治学
An Analysis of Niccolò Machiavelli's *The Prince*	解析尼科洛·马基雅维利《君主论》	政治学
An Analysis of Karl Marx's *Capital*	解析卡尔·马克思《资本论》	政治学
An Analysis of Benedict Anderson's *Imagined Communities*	解析本尼迪克特·安德森《想象的共同体》	政治学
An Analysis of Samuel P. Huntington's *The Clash of Civilizations and the Remaking of World Order*	解析塞缪尔·P.亨廷顿《文明的冲突与世界秩序重建》	政治学
An Analysis of Alexis de Tocqueville's *Democracy in America*	解析阿列克西·德·托克维尔《论美国的民主》	政治学
An Analysis of J. A. Hobson's *Imperialism: A Study*	解析约·阿·霍布森《帝国主义》	政治学
An Analysis of Thomas Paine's *Common Sense*	解析托马斯·潘恩《常识》	政治学
An Analysis of John Rawls's *A Theory of Justice*	解析约翰·罗尔斯《正义论》	政治学
An Analysis of Francis Fukuyama's *The End of History and the Last Man*	解析弗朗西斯·福山《历史的终结与最后的人》	政治学
An Analysis of John Locke's *Two Treatises of Government*	解析约翰·洛克《政府论》	政治学
An Analysis of Sun Tzu's *The Art of War*	解析孙武《孙子兵法》	政治学
An Analysis of Henry Kissinger's *World Order: Reflections on the Character of Nations and the Course of History*	解析亨利·基辛格《世界秩序》	政治学
An Analysis of Jean-Jacques Rousseau's *The Social Contract*	解析让-雅克·卢梭《社会契约论》	政治学

An Analysis of Odd Arne Westad's *The Global Cold War: Third World Interventions and the Making of Our Times*	解析文安立《全球冷战：美苏对第三世界的干涉与当代世界的形成》	政治学
An Analysis of Sigmund Freud's *The Interpretation of Dreams*	解析西格蒙德·弗洛伊德《梦的解析》	心理学
An Analysis of William James' *The Principles of Psychology*	解析威廉·詹姆斯《心理学原理》	心理学
An Analysis of Philip Zimbardo's *The Lucifer Effect*	解析菲利普·津巴多《路西法效应》	心理学
An Analysis of Leon Festinger's *A Theory of Cognitive Dissonance*	解析利昂·费斯汀格《认知失调论》	心理学
An Analysis of Richard H. Thaler & Cass R. Sunstein's *Nudge: Improving Decisions about Health, Wealth, and Happiness*	解析理查德·H.泰勒/卡斯·R.桑斯坦《助推：如何做出有关健康、财富和幸福的更优决策》	心理学
An Analysis of Gordon Allport's *The Nature of Prejudice*	解析高尔登·奥尔波特《偏见的本质》	心理学
An Analysis of Steven Pinker's *The Better Angels of Our Nature: Why Violence Has Declined*	解析斯蒂芬·平克《人性中的善良天使：暴力为什么会减少》	心理学
An Analysis of Stanley Milgram's *Obedience to Authority*	解析斯坦利·米尔格拉姆《对权威的服从》	心理学
An Analysis of Betty Friedan's *The Feminine Mystique*	解析贝蒂·弗里丹《女性的奥秘》	心理学
An Analysis of David Riesman's *The Lonely Crowd: A Study of the Changing American Character*	解析大卫·理斯曼《孤独的人群：美国人社会性格演变之研究》	社会学
An Analysis of Franz Boas's *Race, Language and Culture*	解析弗朗兹·博厄斯《种族、语言与文化》	社会学
An Analysis of Pierre Bourdieu's *Outline of a Theory of Practice*	解析皮埃尔·布尔迪厄《实践理论大纲》	社会学
An Analysis of Max Weber's *The Protestant Ethic and the Spirit of Capitalism*	解析马克斯·韦伯《新教伦理与资本主义精神》	社会学
An Analysis of Jane Jacobs's *The Death and Life of Great American Cities*	解析简·雅各布斯《美国大城市的死与生》	社会学
An Analysis of C. Wright Mills's *The Sociological Imagination*	解析C.赖特·米尔斯《社会学的想象力》	社会学
An Analysis of Robert E. Lucas Jr.'s *Why Doesn't Capital Flow from Rich to Poor Countries?*	解析小罗伯特·E.卢卡斯《为何资本不从富国流向穷国？》	社会学

An Analysis of Émile Durkheim's *On Suicide*	解析埃米尔·迪尔凯姆《自杀论》	社会学
An Analysis of Eric Hoffer's *The True Believer: Thoughts on the Nature of Mass Movements*	解析埃里克·霍弗《狂热分子：群众运动圣经》	社会学
An Analysis of Jared M. Diamond's *Collapse: How Societies Choose to Fail or Survive*	解析贾雷德·M.戴蒙德《大崩溃：社会如何选择兴亡》	社会学
An Analysis of Michel Foucault's *The History of Sexuality Vol. 1: The Will to Knowledge*	解析米歇尔·福柯《性史（第一卷）：求知意志》	社会学
An Analysis of Michel Foucault's *Discipline and Punish*	解析米歇尔·福柯《规训与惩罚》	社会学
An Analysis of Richard Dawkins's *The Selfish Gene*	解析理查德·道金斯《自私的基因》	社会学
An Analysis of Antonio Gramsci's *Prison Notebooks*	解析安东尼奥·葛兰西《狱中札记》	社会学
An Analysis of Augustine's *Confessions*	解析奥古斯丁《忏悔录》	神学
An Analysis of C. S. Lewis's *The Abolition of Man*	解析C.S.路易斯《人之废》	神学

图书在版编目（CIP）数据

解析弗吉尼亚·伍尔芙《一间自己的房间》：汉、英/菲奥娜·鲁滨逊（Fiona Robinson），蒂姆·史密斯–莱恩（Tim Smith-Laing）著；查诗怡译.
—上海：上海外语教育出版社，2019
（世界思想宝库钥匙丛书）
ISBN 978-7-5446-5809-6

Ⅰ.①解… Ⅱ.①菲… ②蒂… ③查… Ⅲ.①伍尔芙（Woolf, Virginia 1882-1941）—妇女文学—文学评论—汉、英 Ⅳ.①I561.065

中国版本图书馆CIP数据核字（2019）第076542号

This Chinese-English bilingual edition of *An Analysis of Virginia Woolf's* A Room of One's Own is published by arrangement with Macat International Limited.
Licensed for sale throughout the world.
本书汉英双语版由Macat国际有限公司授权上海外语教育出版社有限公司出版。
供在全世界范围内发行、销售。

图字：09-2018-549

出版发行：**上海外语教育出版社**
　　　　　（上海外国语大学内）　邮编：200083
电　　话：021-65425300（总机）
电子邮箱：bookinfo@sflep.com.cn
网　　址：http://www.sflep.com
责任编辑：杨莹雪

印　　刷：**上海信老印刷厂**
开　　本：890×1240　1/32　印张5.75　字数118千字
版　　次：2019年8月第1版　2019年8月第1次印刷
印　　数：2 100册

书　　号：ISBN 978-7-5446-5809-6 / I
定　　价：**30.00**元

本版图书如有印装质量问题，可向本社调换
质量服务热线：4008-213-263　电子邮箱：**editorial@sflep.com**